PENGUIN BOOKS

9 TO 5: THE WORKING WOMAN'S GUIDE TO OFFICE SURVIVAL

Ellen Cassedy and Karen Nussbaum are among the ten women who founded the first chapter of 9 to 5, National Association of Working Women, in Boston, when they were both clerk-typists. They have spent the past ten years working with women office workers to win rights and respect in the office.

Ellen Cassedy develops and runs training sessions on career planning and organizing for women workers. She edits the *9 to 5 Newsletter* and directs 9 to 5's research and educational programs. She lives in Philadelphia with her husband and son.

Karen Nussbaum speaks frequently to a broad range of audiences—from office workers to managers—about the concerns of working women. She is the executive director of 9 to 5 and the president of 9 to 5's sister union, District 925 of the Service Employees International Union. She lives in Cleveland with her husband and son.

9 to 5, National Association of Working Women, is headquartered in Cleveland, Ohio, and has members in every state.

THE WORKING WOMAN'S GUIDE TO OFFICE SURVIVAL

by
Ellen Cassedy
and
Karen Nussbaum

Foreword by JANE FONDA

PENGUIN BOOKS

Penguin Books Ltd, Harmondsworth,
Middlesex, England
Penguin Books, 40 West 23rd Street,
New York, New York 10010, U.S.A.
Penguin Books Australia Ltd, Ringwood,
Victoria, Australia
Penguin Books Canada Limited, 2801 John Street,
Markham, Ontario, Canada L3R 1B4
Penguin Books (N.Z.) Ltd, 182–190 Wairau Road,
Auckland 10, New Zealand

First published 1983

LIBRARY OF CONGRESS CATALOGING IN PUBLICATION DATA
Cassedy, Ellen.
9 to 5: the working woman's guide to office survival.
1. Secretaries. 2. Women clerks. 3. Sex discrimination
against women. 4. Sex discrimination in employment.
I. Nussbaum, Karen. II. Title. III. Title: Nine to five.
HF5547.5.C36 1983   650.1'4'024042   83–12173
ISBN 0 14 00.6751 5

Printed in the United States of America by
R. R. Donnelley & Sons Company, Harrisonburg, Virginia
Set in Aster
Designed by Debby Jay

The names of the working women whose stories and words
are used throughout this book have been changed to assure
anonymity.

To those who have built 9 to 5, National Association of Working Women, and to those who will help it grow in the future

Contents

Acknowledgments

ABOVE all, we are grateful to the many women who shared their experiences with us—both 9 to 5 members and others like them. Their tales of unfair office practices appear throughout the book, and their courageous attempts to change management policies form the basis for the advice presented here.

We would also like to thank the following individuals for their advice and support: Ray Abernathy, Eve Berton, Janice Blood, Jeff Blum, Sylvia Cassedy, Richard Cordtz, Kathryn Court, Judith Gregory, Charles Guerrier, Ellen Levine, Denise Mitchell, Anne Moss, Maureen O'Donnell, Diana Roose, Jacquelynn Ruff, Janet Selcer, Jeanne Stellman, John Sweeney, Elaine Taber, Audrey Taylor, Robert Welsh, and Barbara Wertheimer.

The following organizations have also been helpful: the Coalition of Labor Union Women, the Disability Rights Education and Defense Fund, the Pension Rights Center, the Service Employees International Union, the Women's Occupational Health Resource Center, and the Working Women Institute.

Foreword

by Jane Fonda

I'VE worked for nearly twenty-five years. During that time I have known many working women, including women who work in offices in the movie industry. I did a short stint as an office worker myself, but my understanding of the women who work from 9 to 5 has come chiefly through my friendship with Karen Nussbaum.

Over the past ten years, Karen has kept me informed of the development of 9 to 5, National Association of Working Women, and of the growth of the 9 to 5 movement. It was Karen who told me that office work is the largest job category in the country—and one of the lowest paid. She told me about office workers' ongoing quest for career opportunities, for freedom from sexual harassment, for the opportunity to use their skills and abilities. She told me about the growing determination among office workers—a determination to be treated with respect and fairness.

I was so moved by the stories she told me about the members of 9 to 5 that I decided to see for myself. One fall I toured the country, meeting with office workers in groups both large and small—a thousand secretaries in a mass meeting in New York, three older women for an hour's conversation in Boston, thirty office workers in a spirited session over wine and cheese in Cleveland. As these women talked to me about their lives, I couldn't believe what I heard.

A woman who had been at her job for fifteen years said that men she had trained had been promoted to become her superiors. A woman who worked at one of the wealthiest banks in town told of being paid so little that she was eligible for food stamps. Another told of returning from her vacation to find that her boss had decided she was too old and would have to go. Another woman talked of being "plugged in" to her word-processing machine in the morning and finishing work in the evening with such severe eyestrain that she couldn't read the newspaper when she got home. Many told of being treated as nonpeople, of the toll such treatment took on their self-respect. One young woman from Boston said that whenever she was asked what she did for a living, she found herself mumbling, trying to avoid the word "secretary."

I came to understand that office work is hard work and that it is skilled work, and that maybe you could run a business without a boss, but you certainly couldn't run it without office workers.

The result of my research was that I made a movie called *Nine to Five*, after the organization founded by the authors of this book. Judy Bernly, the character I played, was one of the most enjoyable roles of my career. She was patterned after a woman I had met on my travels—a woman with three children who was suddenly thrust into the job market when her husband divorced her without warning. It was a great pleasure playing the role of Judy as she began her first office job and developed the ability to stand up for herself.

Industry moguls were skeptical about the prospects of a movie about secretaries. But *Nine to Five*, which paid more attention to the concerns of the office worker than had the previous twenty-five years of movies put together, was a record-breaking box-office hit.

The movie is a comedy in which a group of secretaries kidnap their boss and take over the office. They keep things running so smoothly that no one realizes the boss is missing. And while he's gone, they take matters into their own hands, revamping corporate policies and improving their working conditions.

Nine to Five was only a fantasy, but this book will help you change your working life.

To be treated with dignity and respect, to earn a decent wage, to be told what is expected of you on the job, to have the opportunity to advance, to enjoy working conditions that do not threaten your health—these are reasonable demands.

The problems you face are serious and widespread. As office workers, you have the power of numbers. Use it—join with your fellow employees and other office workers. Consider joining 9 to 5, National Association of Working Women, using the membership form at the back of this book. Or join the 9 to 5 union, District 925 of the Service Employees International Union, which is winning better pay and working conditions for office workers across the country. There was a time when I had no interest in any organization and was an adamant "nonjoiner." Today I see no more effective way to bring about change than to join an organization.

The struggle for job rights may not be easy, but the rewards will be great. The young woman who was ashamed to tell people what she did for a living went on to say, "I hope I live to see the day when I can raise my head with pride and say, 'I am a secretary; I am an office worker.'"

Introduction

A company once tried to sell office equipment by advertising "This machine is just like your secretary: silent, efficient, and easily manipulable." Those days are over. There is a new spirit in the office.

A movement is afoot. All over the country, women office workers are demanding equal pay, fair promotion opportunity, decent working conditions, and respect. What is happening? How did it all begin?

For us, it began when we were twenty years old and clerk-typists at Harvard University. One day Karen was staggering down the hall carrying a load of doctoral dissertations. "Why aren't you smiling, dear?" asked a passing professor with a wink. Another day Ellen's boss ceremoniously placed a note on her desk before disappearing back into his office. "Please remove calendar from my wall," it said. Ellen went to his office, unstuck two pieces of masking tape from the calendar, and put it on his desk. Why had he wasted his time ordering her to do something that he could have done himself in ten seconds?

Then one afternoon a young male student came into our office. Standing in front of Karen and looking directly at her, he asked, "Isn't anyone here?" At that moment, we realized what it was that our working lives lacked. It was respect. The lack of respect was as commonplace as paper clips. So routine, in fact, that we wondered if there was something wrong with *us* in finding such treatment objectionable.

It wasn't long before we discovered that our own experience was very similar to that of other women office workers. In 1972 we attended a weekend workshop for office workers at the YWCA. As the conference got rolling, the problems poured out. Whatever the industry or the size of the office, women faced a lack of respect, low pay, limited advancement opportunity, and little say over working conditions.

Ellen's story about the calendar was matched and topped by story after story about women required to perform favors for their bosses, cover for them, do their work. One woman complained that her years of experience seemed to be standing in the way of advancement rather than helping her get ahead. Another said she'd gone to college but found that her education hadn't helped her get a better job.

Many complained that they performed duties that were far outside their job descriptions, to which others responded that they wished they *had* job descriptions. An insurance worker said she was doing the same work as the men in her office but was being paid less. Several women said they had trained men to be their own supervisors.

For others, the problems weren't particularly dramatic. They just worked 35 or 40 hours a week, and worked hard, but didn't bring home enough money. A teller said she didn't make enough to get a loan from the bank she worked for. A clerk in a hospital couldn't afford to get sick; a university secretary couldn't afford to send her children to college.

For a few of us, an office job was a way to make a living temporarily, until marriage or until we went back to school. But for most, office work was a lifetime career. And it wasn't necessarily the jobs themselves that we wanted changed. For the most part, we liked our jobs. We liked the variety, the contact with people. We liked being at the hub of the company and knowing what was going on. We liked communicating by phone, in writing, in person. We liked using our initiative, judgment, and diplomatic skills. We were proud of our work. What we didn't like was the way we were treated and how little we were paid.

A consensus grew in our little seminar: We were being taken advantage of, and it was time to put a stop to it. Ten of us got together after the workshop and printed a short newsletter about the issues that frustrated us most. Before work, we stood at subway exits and in front of Boston's biggest office buildings and distributed it to the women hurrying to their jobs. The response was overwhelming. We received dozens of letters and phone calls, and soon held a meeting attended by 300 women, all bursting with grievances about their work situations.

A few months later, in November 1973, we formed an association of working women and called it 9 to 5, after the usual hours of the business day. And if we had thought there was a crying need for such an organization, we became even more convinced when we went to the library for statistics to back up our claims of unfair working conditions.

The situation was much worse than we'd realized. According to the Department of Labor, clerical workers earned less on the average than every kind of blue-collar worker. Women workers earned only a fraction of men's pay in every occupation, and worse yet, that fraction had diminished over the past generation. Within the realm of office work, we averaged $5,000 less per year than men.

We were also surprised to find out from the Department of Labor that office workers were—and are—the largest and fastest-growing sector of the work force. When most people are asked to picture the typical American worker, a man with a lunch pail comes to mind. Yet in fact the typical American worker is a woman at a keyboard. There are nearly 20 million of us, accounting for more than one out of every five workers. Office industries are growing and thriving, and the demand for our labor is healthy. All these conditions increase our chances of winning better treatment.

The movement began to grow. When a business journal carried a brief mention of the organization, we were flooded with over 3,000 calls and letters from secretaries all over the country. Some spoke in whispers; one woman said her boss had threatened to fire her if she joined. ("So I *had* to call," she explained.) We learned of women taking action all over the country, in the smallest, most out-of-the-way places. Eight bank workers in a tiny, conservative Midwestern town went on strike for eighteen long, cold months after the bank president told them, "We're not all equal, you know." Their story became national news. We were contacted by a woman in a small Southern town who had overheard a young man boasting that his salary exceeded hers. She and her coworkers filed charges and won the largest back-pay settlement in the state's civil rights history.

We joined forces with women workers organizing in other cities. We answered letters about job problems and held workshops on how to ask for a raise, plan for retirement, and organize to win better treatment. The news of victories began to roll in. Women reported that they had asked for raises for the first time in their lives—and gotten them. Petitions were circulated. Groups of women met with their bosses to demand policy changes. Women rewrote their job descriptions to make them more accurate, and stopped making coffee. Women in the publishing, insurance, and banking industries filed discrimination charges and won millions of dollars in back pay as well as new promotion and training programs.

National Secretaries' Week, established in 1952 by the U.S. Department of Commerce, underwent a radical transformation. The last full week in April had been a time when bosses were supposed to present their secretaries with a bouquet of roses or a box of candy in thanks for a year of hard work. Now secretaries used the occasion both to reflect with pride on their contributions and to ask whether they were being fairly compensated. "Raises, not roses" became a nationwide rallying cry.

Office workers began to be visible. Representatives of 9 to 5 were even invited to speak at management conferences. Managers suddenly wanted to know what office workers were thinking. Some began to overhaul their employment policies and make much-needed changes.

To be sure, many bosses dragged their feet and fought back outright when asked to treat office workers better. The Chamber of Commerce of one Southern city even sent out a letter to all its members, inviting them to a training session on how to respond to office workers' demands for grievance procedures and higher pay. But the mailing backfired. Secretaries themselves opened the mail for their bosses, read the letter, and deluged the local 9 to 5 office with applications for membership.

The labor movement became interested in office workers. In 1981, 9 to 5 and the Service Employees International Union jointly established District 925, a nationwide union for office workers. Progress was made in our organizing efforts from Washington, D.C., to Washington State, and office workers from all over the country called for information on organizing a union. (The toll-free number is 202-452-8750.)

Today 9 to 5 is a national association of working women. Women call every day to ask how to join or how to form a local chapter. Some are individuals; others are members of groups that have been meeting for months at a local church or company cafeteria. Our national newsletter is read by typists, administrative assistants, tellers, editors, word-processing operators, secretaries, clerks.

The outlook for women office workers is now vastly different from what it was a decade ago. It is true that the majority of the nation's 42 million working women are still employed in so-called women's jobs. But what has changed dramatically is our ability to win respect and fair treatment. Public opinion is now on our side. We no longer have to spend our time convincing others that discrimination exists, or that women deserve equal pay, fair promotion opportunities, and respect. Along with this new climate, our growing numbers give us strength, and our urgent economic needs give us a compelling reason to take action. And finally, women have realized that we will have to organize to achieve the rights and respect we deserve.

As we prepared to celebrate 9 to 5's tenth anniversary, we looked back over what we had done and saw a need for a book that shared what we had learned about improving our status and working conditions. It is not a book about upward mobility—about how to get out of office work. It is a book for those of us who hold "9 to 5" office jobs, as well as the similar service, sales, and factory jobs that most women perform for the whole of their careers. Many parts of the book will also be useful to men who hold such jobs, and the book may help bosses who want to know how to treat their employees better. (Since the great majority of office workers are women, and most bosses are men, we refer to the office worker as "she" and the boss as "he" throughout the book.)

9 to 5: The Working Woman's Guide to Office Survival contains the most useful material developed by 9 to 5 over the past ten years. It includes material from exercises and handouts used in our after-work seminars; surveys concerning issues such as pay and job stress that were filled out by office workers throughout the country; model employment policies developed by office workers; public policy recommendations prepared for congressional testimony; and reports on office health hazards, economic trends, automation, and the retirement system. The book also draws on stories gathered from our travels, our local chapters, and letters we've received over the years from office workers— stories of outrageous mistreatment by employers and stories of success in revamping office policies. All these stories—however unbelievable—are true.

The first three chapters deal with the core issues: respect, pay, and advancement opportunity. The next three discuss topics that are newer to the office work force: health hazards, the growth of office automation, and issues for working parents. The following chapter will help you begin planning now for a secure retirement. Finally, two chapters describe the important tools we have at our disposal—legal rights and organizing tactics—and the conclusion looks at the future for working women and for the 9 to 5 movement.

We hope *9 to 5: The Working Woman's Guide to Office Survival* will give you the facts you need in order to take an objective look at your situation, stop blaming yourself for your job problems, and take comfort in the fact that you are not alone. We hope you will gain the tools you need to solve those problems for yourself and others, make decisions, take action, and stand up for yourself. And we hope the book will impart a renewed sense of respect for the importance of your work and the means to put this respect into daily practice.

THE WORKING
WOMAN'S GUIDE TO
OFFICE SURVIVAL

1.
A Matter of Respect

They call us girls until the day we retire without pension.
> —*New York office worker*

One day a supervisor in my office was typing his own letter. A dean walked by and laughed: "Boy, some people will stoop to anything."
> —*Boston secretary*

OFFICE work is important work—so important that it is the nation's largest job category. The nearly 20 million of us who work in offices make a crucial contribution to business, government, academia, and social service. It matters that we do our jobs well. For each of us, an office job can and should be a source of pride. But office workers don't receive the respect we deserve. Examples of disrespect are legion.

Many an office worker has complained that she was hired to type and file but instead found herself doing the boss's laundry or driving his sick dog home from the office. There are secretaries who have been asked to clean the boss's dentures, finish his crossword puzzle, mail his urine specimen to the lab, return a pair of his wife's pantyhose to a store. One secretary had to mail a

letter to her boss's neighbor, complaining about a bark-
ing dog. But first she had to drive across the state line in
order to give the letter a mystery postmark. Another
secretary had to place illegal bets for her boss—without
even sharing in the winnings. Still another had to sew
up a hole in her boss's trousers—while he was wearing
them.

Some office workers don't mind getting the coffee or
taking suits to the dry cleaner's. They welcome such an
errand as a chance to get up and walk around. But for
many others, being asked to do personal errands for the
boss feels like an executive power play. It reinforces a
secretarial stereotype that they want no part of.

Some office workers complain that when they're not
running errands, they are treated like children. Insurance workers cite the bells that signal them to be in
their seats at the start of the workday; telephone operators are irked by the "pee list," a waiting list they must
sign when they want to go to the bathroom.

And when employers use the word "girl" to refer to
women office workers, they are probably not taking
their female employees as seriously as they should be.
United Technologies Corporation took aim at this practice with an advertisement in the *Wall Street Journal*
several years ago:

> Wouldn't 1979 be a great year to take one giant step
> forward for womankind and get rid of "the girl"? Your
> attorney says, "If I'm not here just leave it with the girl."
> The purchasing agent says, "Drop off your bid with the
> girl." A manager says, "My girl will get back to your
> girl." *What* girl? Do they mean Miss Rose? Do they mean
> Ms. Torres? Do they mean Mrs. McCullough? Do they
> mean Joy Jackson? "The girl" is certainly a woman
> when she's out of her teens. Like you, she has a name.
> Use it.

We couldn't agree more.

A San Francisco woman described how a particular boss deals with women employees: he leans back in his chair, puts his feet on top of the desk, and proceeds to clip his nails with great concentration. The underling is forced to communicate with the soles of the man's shoes. Another boss silently drops large rush orders on his secretary's desk just as she is tidying up to go home.

And employer insensitivity reached a peak in this incident: a university secretary reports that she was sitting at her desk one day when a coworker burst into the office looking ill and then fell to the floor. A moment later a world-renowned professor opened the door. Without a word, he stepped over the woman's body to get to the file cabinet, retrieved a file, stepped back over her body, and left.

"Many mindless decisions are made by bosses who don't have day-to-day contact with the work," says a Pittsburgh office worker. "The clerical workers know better, but we aren't allowed to exercise our intelligence because it is assumed we have none."

For example, an Illinois law office bought expensive new carpeting and bolted the secretaries' chairs and desks to the floor so the carpet wouldn't be damaged by moving furniture. No one consulted the secretaries about the arrangements, and Monday morning found them unable to reach their phones or typewriters while seated. The firm had to reposition the chairs and desks, creating unsightly holes in the rug.

Some bosses do pay attention to their secretaries, but look upon them as decorative objects rather than skilled workers. As a 1977 typing drill put it, "A secretary is nice to look at. She makes an office a pleasant place with her charm and her knack of adapting to the moods of others." A Cleveland employment agency sent out advertisements luring employers with these offers:

"Secretary: A raven-haired dynamo! Engineering secretary: Blonde-haired, blue-eyed and charismatic!"

Numerous studies show that sexual harassment—defined as any unwelcome sexual advances experienced on the job—is widespread. Surveys by the U.S. government, *Redbook* magazine, and the Working Women Institute found that millions of working women have some experience with sexual harassment, and that many who refuse sexual favors lose a job, promotion, or raise as a result of employer retaliation. Victims of sexual harassment suffer from headaches, depression, ulcers, and even more serious disorders, such as high blood pressure.

Sexual harassment can take the form of suggestive remarks. The group of secretaries whose boss subjects them to a string of off-color jokes is being harassed, as are the clerk whose boss follows her into the file room and "accidentally" brushes against her and the woman whose boss pleads with her to have a drink with him, pins her to her chair, and tries to kiss her.

There are some people in the work world who will never respect you no matter what you do. Your individual conduct may not be enough to overcome racial or sexual prejudice, for example. Some people will not look you straight in the eye once they hear your job title. But if you respect yourself and your skills, you can communicate that self-respect to others. This can be the first step toward being treated with respect.

When you are not sufficiently respected at work, it can be hard to remember that you are a talented and competent person. The following exercises can help to remind you of your skills and abilities. They can provide the spur you need to ask for the raise, accurate job description, or promotion that will better reflect your contributions to your employer. And they can be useful if you need to write a résumé for a job hunt.

EXERCISE #1: LIFE ACHIEVEMENTS

Give yourself credit for what you have accomplished in your life, both at work and outside of work, including volunteer experiences, school, and hobbies. List accomplishments large and small—a meal you prepared for forty guests, your graduation from high school, a project you completed, a problem you solved.

Next, list the skills you used in these experiences. Try to use the following verbs, which are valued by employers: administer, analyze, compile, conduct, control, coordinate, create, design, develop, direct, evaluate, manage, negotiate, operate, organize, prepare, produce, purchase, train.

One woman analyzed what she had done in organizing a double-wedding reception for 300 people. Recognizing her ability to coordinate, create, design, direct, manage, prepare, and purchase, she gained the confidence to apply for a promotion to office manager.

EXERCISE #2: LIST THE SKILLS YOU USE ON YOUR JOB

To make sure your list is complete, you may find it useful to keep a job diary in which you write down everything you do at work for a week. In addition to typing, filing, and answering the telephone, remember to make note of such skills as organizing a filing system, screening information so it can be handled by others, interviewing clients and ascertaining their needs, composing letters, planning how and when a project will be handled. Again, use action verbs.

Secretaries at an insurance company on the West Coast circulated and filled out questionnaires about their job duties. The results showed that each of them was functioning not just as a secretary but also as a salesperson, underwriter, claims adjuster, office manager, and mail clerk! Why, they wondered, were they earning only a small fraction of the average insurance agent's salary?

Respecting yourself and your skills is one step toward being treated with respect by your employer, but it is only a step. Respect for women office workers as a group will come through the collective and individual actions of thousands of us who insist upon being treated fairly from day to day. To combat the disrespectful attitudes and behavior you encounter in the work world, you must speak up and take action.

SPEAK UP TO COMBAT INVISIBILITY

"Recently I was working at my desk when my boss took a new employee around to introduce him," says a San Francisco administrative assistant. "He totally ignored me and introduced him to the men. I fumed but couldn't think of what to do. What could I have done?"

In such a situation, don't be immobilized by your employer's rudeness. Casually get up and join the group. At an appropriate moment, introduce yourself to the new employee. Your coworkers will respect your assertiveness, and your boss may get the message.

Speak up if your boss takes you for granted by consistently dropping last-minute tasks on your desk at 4:45. Tell him you'd like as much advance warning as possible; with sufficient notice, you might be able to eliminate the need to stay late. And tell your boss before doing overtime work that you expect to receive time-and-a-half pay. You might also analyze the cause of the rush orders and overtime hours. Could the work be organized more efficiently? If your whole department is being asked to work overtime for a protracted period, you and your coworkers could make a joint proposal to your supervisor.

Speak up if your boss won't recognize your suggestions or your career goals. Try using the "memo strategy" to put them in writing.

Joan Q. tells this story: "I've made several suggestions to my boss for improving operations in my department. Soon afterwards I see him getting the credit. Once I had to type a memo to his boss in which he made *my* suggestion as if it were *his*. Another time he announced my innovation to the clerical staff—without mentioning me."

If this is your problem, make your proposal in writing, in the form of a memo to your boss. Describe how your ideas will benefit the company (for example, by increasing efficiency, improving morale, or saving money), suggest a timetable, and ask if your boss will work with you to develop your proposal for presentation to his superiors. Make it clear that you want the proposal submitted in both your names. And keep a copy of your memo for use at evaluation and raise time.

Helen B. says, "I've told my boss repeatedly that I'm interested in being trained for some of the new positions that are opening up in the department, but he isn't listening. He's never told me he won't promote me, but he keeps hiring people—mostly men—from outside the company."

If this happens to you, you need to meet with your boss to discuss your career goals. Immediately after the meeting, write him a memo (see the sample) and keep a copy. If there is no action in the agreed-upon time period, follow up with another memo. If your boss remains

February 2, 19____

Dear Mr. D.,
   This is my recollection of our meeting yesterday:
   I said that I am interested in being promoted to the position of editorial assistant. A position may open up in March. You said that you would give me a chance to review some of the job duties involved in the position, and that you would be sure to interview me this month.
   Thank you.

Helen B.

reluctant to help, ask who has the power to grant your request, and write a memo to that person. Add your memos to your personnel file at your performance review.

SPEAK UP WHEN YOUR PERFORMANCE IS BEING EVALUATED

The performance evaluation is a good time to find out whether your worth is recognized and to make positive changes in the way you are regarded and treated. Ideally, a performance evaluation is carried out by a supervisor who is concerned about your career development and wants to help you overcome your weaknesses and build on your strengths. But since this isn't always the case, you may have to take deliberate steps to make the most of the evaluation process:

   1. *Prepare.* Know when your evaluation will take place and who will review your work. Familiarize yourself with your job description, which is the basis of the review. If possible, get a copy of the written evaluation form and evaluate yourself ahead of time. (See the Sample Performance Evaluation Form.) Assess your

SAMPLE PERFORMANCE EVALUATION FORM

Name of employee _____

Job title _____

Date of employment _____

Department _____

	Unsatis-factory	Below Average	Average	Above Average
1. Quality of work	☐	☐	☐	☐
2. Quantity of work	☐	☐	☐	☐
3. Reliability	☐	☐	☐	☐
4. Use of judgment	☐	☐	☐	☐
5. Initiative	☐	☐	☐	☐
6. Attendance	☐	☐	☐	☐
7. Promptness	☐	☐	☐	☐
8. Response to supervision	☐	☐	☐	☐

Supervisor's comments _____
_____
_____
_____

Supervisor's signature _____Date____

Employee's comments _____
_____
_____
_____

Employee's signature _____Date____

strengths and weaknesses. Compare yourself to others in your job category, if any. What do you do well? What needs improvement? Does your job description need updating? What goals would you set for yourself over the next year?

2. *Anticipate.* Don't wait for evaluation time; discuss your progress regularly with your boss. Clear up misunderstandings and discuss problems that may be brewing. Add memos about these discussions to your file.

3. *At the review.* Take an active, positive role. Help your boss become more conscious of your strong points and ask for specific suggestions on how to improve in your weaker areas.

If you receive a negative review, do not react hastily. Consult friends and associates before you respond. Then ask for another meeting to request documentation for your boss's claims. Review your job description and the evaluation criteria with your boss. Add your own side of the story in writing to your file; be straightforward and brief.

Remember that not every unfavorable review is unfair. Make an extra effort to receive ongoing evaluation of your progress toward correcting the problems. Your next review could be much better if you do.

SPEAK UP TO CHANGE YOUR BOSS'S PERSONAL-ERRANDS POLICY

Suggest this model to your employer in a memo or at a meeting:

- Only company-related duties should be required. (No typing of children's school reports, buying of anniversary cards, and so on.)
- An employee should be asked if she is willing to

perform duties that are not strictly related to her job and should have the opportunity to refuse.

- Matters that affect the comfort of the whole office staff should either be put in one person's job description and fairly compensated or be shared among staff members without regard to sex.
- All required duties should be listed in the job description.
- Company management should issue and enforce a standard policy to this effect.

And learn to say no firmly but without hostility. Try using these lines:

- My work on the XYZ project comes first. I'd like to be sure I'm caught up on it before taking on your son's term paper.
- I'd rather do some other company work if I have extra time. For example, I'm interested in learning to do _____.
- I prefer not to do noncompany work on company time. I feel I owe it to both my career and my company.
- I'll make the coffee today. But I feel that since it's a personal matter that we all share, everyone should pitch in.
- I know I've been getting your sandwich for eighteen years, but now it's begun to bother me. I'd rather not do it every day. Please check to see whether I'm busy before putting your lunch money on my desk.

Here are several ways in which women have dealt successfully with the issue of personal errands:

After five years as a secretary to a bank vice-president, Diane P. found that her services as coffee maker and caterer had mushroomed to such an extent that she had difficulty attending to the secretarial duties listed in her job description. She brewed and delivered as many as ten pots of coffee a day and prepared and cleaned up lunches for fifteen people.

Diane wrote a memo to her boss: "Effective Monday, March 6, I will no longer, under any circumstances, perform the aforementioned kitchen and domestic duties." The memo closed with an invitation to discuss the problem and reach a "fair and equitable solution."

Diane and her boss had a calm, civilized conversation after she convinced him it was not a laughing matter. "I do not have to make the coffee anymore," she reported later. "My taking a stand changed his attitude quite a bit. He's developed a new respect for me, and we have a better working relationship as a result."

Loretta G.'s boss kept her busy with a variety of errands unrelated to her position as a secretary at an imports firm. When he asked her to pack his suitcase for a trip to the Far East, she'd had enough.

Upon his return, she told him she felt that duties unrelated to her job were taking up too much of her time. She presented her boss with the draft of a job description she had drawn up and asked if there were other duties that should be added. He lacked the nerve to add valet duties to a written job description and stopped requiring them after this discussion.

When Liz P. was fired from her job as a proofreader for refusing to serve the boss his lunch and clean up after him, she fought back by filing a discrimination charge with the Equal Employment Opportunity Commission (EEOC).

"Did the men have to serve lunch? Of course not," Liz commented. "When I asked the bookkeeper how she decided who was to participate in serving lunch, she said, 'By whoever's female, of course.'

"An EEOC representative drew up a draft of an agreement with my former employer: that I be awarded back pay for the time it took me to find a new job, that my personnel file be cleared, and that the company cease the practice of having someone serve lunch to the president.

"The company agreed to the first proposals but said that the company president *had* to be served his lunch. An alternative was worked out: the duty would be shared by the company's clerical staff (five men and five women) and the EEOC would monitor this arrangement."

SPEAK UP TO STOP SEXUAL HARASSMENT

If you are experiencing harassment, take action immediately. Recognize that you are faced with a situation that can damage your health, confidence, and career. Look for emotional support from someone who can understand your predicament—a friend, relative, coworker.

1. *Inform the harasser that his attentions are unwanted.* "Mr. _____, I don't like your touching me. Now that you know I don't like it, please stop." Tell the harasser that you don't mix your private life and business life. Refuse all invitations firmly. Speak with conviction. Don't play along or try to call his bluff. And don't be afraid of rejecting him—he can take it.

If harassment continues, *write a memo* and keep a copy: "Dear Mr. _____, It makes me very uncomfortable when you touch me and ask me personal questions. Now that you are aware that your attention is unwanted, I am certain you will stop."

2. *Keep a written record* of the harassment, with date, time, place, witnesses, and your response. Be explicit. Also keep copies of any memos or correspondence that attest to the quality of your work; your boss may question your job performance if you refuse his attentions.

3. *Look for witnesses*, other victims, and further evidence. A woman who is harassed often finds that her coworkers have been as well. Sexual harassment is not confined to women of a particular race, age, marital status, or life-style. Two accusations of harassment are much harder to ignore than one.

4. *Use in-company grievance procedures*, if any, and give your employer an opportunity to rectify the situation before pursuing a legal strategy, such as filing a charge or suit. If you are represented by a union, consider filing a grievance.

5. *If you need to take further legal action*, call a legal service agency, your state discrimination agency, or the Equal Employment Opportunity Commission. Sexual harassment is illegal if it interferes with your work or creates an intimidating or offensive work environment, or if your job or promotion depends on your submission. (See Chapter 8.)

SPEAK UP AS A GROUP

Forming a support group with your coworkers may be the most effective way to command the respect of your employer and get rid of policies that denigrate women.

For example, when Toni S. was fired from her job at a small Midwestern firm for refusing to make coffee, a group of office workers descended on the firm during the lunch hour, armed with an "Executive's Guide to Making Your Own Coffee." The guide included complete instructions on how to use a coffee vending machine (including how to insert a coin and select cream and sugar) and went on to describe how to fill an electric coffee maker with water and coffee. Toni got her job back.

A staff association at a Canadian university formally negotiated a contract clause allowing members to file a grievance if they were asked to "perform duties of a personal nature not connected with the approved operations of the university."

Such issues—who makes the coffee, who is addressed by her first name—are both important on a personal level and symbolic of the larger concern about how women are regarded in our society. But respect for the office worker must go beyond office etiquette. Fair pay, opportunities for career mobility, safe working conditions, and decent retirement policies are the building blocks of the respectful treatment that we must insist upon.

2.
How to Get Paid What You're Worth

I work full time at an insurance company, but I earn so little that I am eligible for food stamps. My boss gives me time off to pick up my check at the welfare office, but he won't raise my salary.

—Seattle office worker

When I asked for a raise, my boss suggested I see a psychiatrist.

—Chicago bank secretary

I N the nineteenth century, an office job was a plum. Most office workers were men, often the sons or nephews of their employers, and many were being trained to take over the firm one day. The work was safe and clean, and it paid better than factory jobs.

Today office work has mushroomed to become the largest job category in the country, and most office workers are women. Office pay has fallen behind that of heavily unionized industrial workers. In the words of AFL-CIO official Elmer Chatak, office workers in the finance industries are "twenty years behind industrial workers in wages and benefits."

Within office work as a whole, women average $5,616 less per year than men, according to the Department of

Labor. Indeed, in every occupation, clerical and non-clerical, women fare poorly compared with their male counterparts. Overall, for every dollar men earn, women earn only 59¢. And a 1980 United Nations study stated that women do two-thirds of the world's work for only one-tenth of the world's pay.

Our low pay is not the result of a lack of education, skills, or experience. The U.S. Commission on Civil Rights has documented that a huge pay gap between men and women remains even when we compare individuals with similar education, training, and work history.

Why do we earn so little? First, women tend to work in industries that are not heavily unionized, and this lack of organization takes its toll on our pay.

And part of the explanation lies in the concentration of women in lower-level jobs. Most of us work in jobs occupied chiefly by women. For example, 96% of the typists, 95% of the nurses, and 99% of the secretaries in this country are women. "Women's jobs" are stereotyped as being less valuable than men's. "The more an occupation is dominated by women, the less it pays," concluded a 1981 study by the National Academy of Sciences.

Few office workers are aware that a widespread practice of wage-fixing also holds down women office workers' pay. While your employer makes a great show of salary secrecy within the company, he may be comparing notes on the size of your raise with scores of supposedly competitive firms in the city.

In one large Eastern city, for example, 9 to 5 discovered that a group of major clerical employers had published a confidential survey of the wages and benefits paid by member companies and was meeting regularly to discuss it. The state attorney general investigated the group, concerned that it might be acting as a monopoly by fixing low annual raises and curbing office workers' bargaining power. The result was some restriction of the group's activities.

In cities from coast to coast, women have challenged these semisecret consortia. Nonetheless, urban bosses are still getting together to undercut office workers' bargaining power. When your boss tells you, "It's out of my hands—I have to pay the going rate," you might ask yourself who establishes the going rate.

If office workers as a whole are poorly paid, it's not because our work is not valuable to our employers. The emerging concept of "pay equity" is establishing that office work is worth far more than it pays. Advocates of pay equity, or equal pay for work of comparable worth, are taking aim at the practice of paying women less than men for jobs of equal value—i.e., jobs that require comparable skill, effort, responsibility, and working conditions.

When the Equal Pay Act was enacted in 1963, many believed that women workers would soon be paid as much as men. Unfortunately this did not happen. The act said that women and men who did the same work at the same workplace must be paid equally, but that left many underpaid women out in the cold. Few women office workers work side by side with men with whom they can compare themselves.

So despite the Equal Pay Act, the wage gap has persisted and even widened, largely because of the concentration of women in a small number of low-paying occupations. To outlaw the practice of undervaluing whole job categories of women and bring the spirit of the Equal Pay Act to these women's jobs, employers should be required to raise wages for jobs that have been downgraded through sex discrimination.

In one county, for example, schoolteachers (who are

mostly women) with college degrees receive a starting salary below that of liquor-store clerks (who are mostly men) with no college education. Nurses and office workers are often paid less than parking lot attendants, janitors, and other workers in less-skilled jobs dominated by men. One major company posted these two openings, the first for a job held mostly by women, the second mostly by men:

Position: *General Clerk*
DUTIES: Maintains accounting cost records; processes records; processes and balances statistical and expense reports; researches material and projects budget; types correspondence and various statistical reports, technical manuals, purchase orders and equipment records; analyzes invoices and determines allocation of charges to be expensed or capitalized; assists accounting clerk in maintaining records and accounting procedures; answers telephone, takes messages and service calls information.
ABILITIES: Excellent statistical and figure aptitude required to compile information, assemble figures and reports, compute and maintain data. General knowledge of accounting and purchasing payables procedures. Must be well organized and able to work independently. Accurate statistical typing. Ability to demonstrate good judgment. Excellent telephone etiquette. Budget and expense experience would be helpful.
SALARY: $745–$1,090

Position: *Shipping and Receiving Clerk*
DUTIES: Perform shipping and receiving duties in the furniture department; receive incoming shipments; assist in unloading; store and deliver items to appropriate location.
ABILITIES: Able to lift equipment in excess of 100 pounds; legible handwriting; no condition or illness which may affect ability to do the job.
SALARY: $1,030–$1,100

Employers who oppose pay equity say that comparing such jobs is like comparing apples and oranges, and that "the marketplace" should determine wages. They also cite the high cost of correcting for past discrimination.

But for years employers have been comparing one job with another as they assign wages within their firms. "The marketplace" may reflect nothing but past and present discrimination by other employers. And many studies, as well as the experience of other countries, show that the cost of pay equity would not be exorbitant, particularly if the changes were phased in gradually. Moreover, if it costs money to treat women like first-class citizens, then that is a cost that must be paid. In the long run, fully recognizing the talents of women will benefit our society far more than undervaluing us has done.

In the past five years, many employers and public jurisdictions (cities, counties, and states) have commissioned studies to determine whether the salaries of female-dominated jobs accurately reflect their value to the employer, or whether these salaries are depressed simply because women fill the jobs. In performing an "equity" job evaluation, experts use procedures developed long before this issue arose—procedures that are part of standard management practice. They begin by reviewing or creating job descriptions for every position in the organization. Each job is then assigned points based on the level of skill, educational background, effort, responsibility, and the difficulty of the working conditions.

The position of executive secretary, for example, is assigned high points for such skills as typing, taking dictation, and dealing diplomatically with clients. If a business education is a requirement for the position, additional points are assigned. High points are assigned for effort and responsibility because the job is a busy and demanding one, and failure to do it well would result in lost revenues, poor corporate image, inconvenience to clients, and so on. Depending on the situation, the job might also be allotted points for such difficult working conditions as constant interruptions, frequent overtime, stress, and restricted movement.

Next—and this is the innovative step—jobs with similar numbers of points are compared to see whether a "woman's job" with 200 points, for instance, pays the same as a "man's job" with 200 points.

These studies have concluded that clerical jobs are equal to many men's jobs in skill, education, effort, responsibility, and even physical demands. Further, they have found that clerical workers are typically underpaid by more than 40%. In a study commissioned by Washington State, for example, secretaries were rated the same as maintenance electricians in a job skills survey, but the secretaries were paid 45% less than the electricians.

The principle of pay equity is gaining widespread acceptance. The Supreme Court opened the door on the issue in 1981 in the *Gunther* case, supporting four Oregon prison matrons who filed a discrimination suit. The women argued that although their jobs had been evaluated at 95% of the male prison guards' "worth," they were paid only 70% as much as the men. Other court rulings have also favored the plaintiffs, and many other cases are pending.

Unions have also advanced the cause of pay equity, using the principle to upgrade the salaries of their members. In 1981 San Jose, California, city workers won the first successful strike over equal pay for comparable work. The strikers pointed out that the mayor's own

secretary had been ranked equal in skills and responsibility to a senior air-conditioning mechanic but was
paid 42% less. The employees gained a total of $1.5
million in equity raises.

Office employers can often afford to pay more. Millions of office workers are employed in the finance industries, which rarely have trouble turning a profit. And
other industries, too, can find money for raises when
they decide they need to. In the midst of the 1981 reces-
sion, for example, executive salaries rose an average of
15.9%.

Even in hard times, when office workers have pressed
for higher pay, they have often succeeded in getting it.
One Los Angeles secretary prepared a check to pay for
the lunches of fourteen people entertained by her boss.
The bill came to an unbelievable $240 per person—more
than her weekly salary. She asked for a raise and got it.
Office workers in Baltimore started a "Clean Up Banking" campaign to publicize and upgrade the low wages
of women who work in banks. Through public pressure,
including rallies on the steps of four major banks, they
won millions of dollars in raises.

So don't feel selfish, presumptuous, or overly aggressive when you demand more money. Chances are the
money is there, and you deserve it. Your employer may
even be waiting for you to ask, as in the case of Gwen S.,
a California secretary.

"When I first started working," Gwen said, "I thought
all I had to do was work hard and wait for the raises.
But one day I overheard my supervisor telling a manager, 'I guess she's satisfied. She hasn't asked for a raise.' I
won't make that mistake again."

Maria N., office manager and mother of five, applied
for a new job. "They made me a salary offer which was
actually higher than I had set in my own mind. Then I

thought, Why am I shortchanging myself? I'm minimizing my own ability and my contributions to an organization when I say, 'OK, I can settle for less because I'm not the sole wage earner.'

"I said that the job entailed many more responsibilities than I'd had previously and that we should renegotiate the salary. They were quite willing to do so. The salary I ended up with was a lot higher than the original offer.

"I'd never pushed like that before. I was quite proud of myself."

Office workers as a group are due for a raise. To get paid what we're worth, we need to develop our bargaining power and use it on a grand scale. In addition, when you ask for a raise as an individual, you can strengthen your bargaining position through careful preparation, negotiation, followthrough, and good timing.

First, find out about salary policies in your office. Consult your supervisor or your personnel handbook or personnel officer. Do increases occur yearly? Are they linked to performance reviews? Or is the raise policy fairly arbitrary, depending on the initiative of individuals? With this information, you can approach your boss before your scheduled increase has been decided upon. (If your increase has already been set, gear your presentation to why you deserve a better raise.)

Have a figure in mind before asking for a raise. Call the Bureau of Labor Statistics (listed in the telephone book under "U.S. Government") for average wage figures for your area, and discuss salaries with your coworkers.

Unless your salary increases to match the rise in the cost of living, you will lose ground. Use this formula to compute what you need just to break even:

a. Current inflation rate: _____%
   (Check with your local Chamber of
   Commerce or Bureau of Labor Sta-
   tistics for updated figures.)

b. Current salary: _____

c. Cost of living increase for your salary
   (a × b):   _____

d. Current salary plus the increase in
   the cost of living (b + c) equals what
   you need to break even: _____

If you are reluctant to discuss your salary with other employees, ask yourself why. "My boss told me that I was making a little more than everyone else and asked me not to mention my salary to anyone," one woman said. "I was afraid the other women would resent me if they knew I was making more than they were."

"I was embarrassed," said another. "I was making much less than I wanted to be, and I didn't want anyone to know how little I had settled for."

Women who overcome the tradition of salary secrecy are often glad they did. One group of women wrote down their salaries and recent raises and tossed the slips of paper into a pile on the lunchroom table. This way they preserved their privacy while getting a sense of the salary range in their department. Several of them were surprised to find that raises they had thought unusually large were actually standard. Talking face to face, they became indignant at how low *all* their salaries were. Their support for one another was helpful when they asked for raises.

While many employers discourage employees from discussing their pay—whether to protect people's feelings or to keep salaries down—others are abandoning the practice. A 1982 *Wall Street Journal* article quoted several managers who feel that posting salary ranges gives employees "something to shoot for" and "improves employee morale." One firm even holds salary seminars to discuss the pay rates of various jobs. (Incidentally, it is illegal to discipline employees for discussing their salaries; such activity is protected under the National Labor Relations Act.)

Having collected the necessary background information, you are ready to compile all the reasons why you deserve a raise. Use the following list as the basis of your presentation.

- Additional job duties you've assumed since you were last reviewed or promoted.
- Newly acquired skills. Did you learn how to use any new equipment in the last year? Implement new procedures?
- The names and dates of any successfully completed special projects. (An office log or appointment book may help you recall dates and events you've forgotten. Whenever possible, ask for a raise just after you've made a significant contribution, not after you've made a big error.)
- Work beyond the call of duty—overtime (paid and unpaid), training new personnel (formally and informally), helping other coworkers, filling in for the boss, and so on.
- Suggestions or revised procedures that have saved the department or company money, or have increased efficiency.
- Any written commendations of you or your work, such as notes of thanks and comments on memos.
- Courses, workshops, or seminars you've attended (including grade received, if any) during the last year.

Now that you have the ammunition to support your request for more money, anticipate the reasons your employer may use to deny you a raise. He will probably try to put off giving increases—he's paid to keep costs down. Preparing to meet his objections will help you to stay calm and remain reasonable. If you are nervous, remind yourself that the worst thing that can happen is that your boss might refuse your request or ask to see you in six months. Give careful thought to the objections he might raise and be ready to counter them. For example:

YOUR BOSS: The budget was decided on last June. There's nothing I can do for you at this time. I'll consider you for a raise, but not for another six months.

YOU: Would you put that in writing for me?

(And make sure you do get a statement, even if you have to write it yourself. In six months, take the statement to your boss.)

YOUR BOSS: Only five percent of the employees in this department can be rated "outstanding" this year. Only a limited number of raises are possible.

YOU: My job performance is outstanding. My job evaluation was a good one.

(If you do not agree with points in the evaluation, document your disagreement in writing.)

YOUR BOSS: What do you need more money for? Men have to support a family—you're only a second income. Your salary is good for a woman [or a person your age, or a single person].

YOU: I expect to be paid according to my work performance regardless of my personal circumstances.

(In some cases it is illegal to assign salaries on the basis of these factors. Your employer may be breaking the law if you're receiving unequal pay for equal work, a lower salary than your male predecessor, or lower pay than men whose jobs are of a lower rank than yours. Speak to your boss or a personnel officer, or consider filing a discrimination charge.)

YOUR BOSS: You're doing a hell of a job; we really love having you here. And we've been so good to you— don't you agree? [These words substitute for the raise.]

YOU: Yes, I do, and a raise will help me continue to be enthusiastic, productive, and a good employee.

YOUR BOSS: I don't have final authority.

YOU: May I have your approval to begin with? If you'll tell me who does have the authority, I'll approach him directly.

YOUR BOSS: I'll see what I can do; trust me.

YOU: Fine. May I get back to you on Wednesday?

(Keep checking back. Be assertive and be persistent.)

Now you're ready to approach your boss for an appointment. For some, this is the hardest part. Frances G. recalls, "I tried out dozens of lines, ranging from 'I need to speak to you about something' to 'Are you busy right now?' to 'I want a raise.' Finally I decided that at the end of his coffee break—a time when I know he tends to be idly flipping through correspondence—I would say these exact words: 'I'd like to make an appointment to talk to you about a raise.' I did it! And I did get my raise."

If possible, arrange to meet in your own office or in a neutral setting, such as a conference room, not in your boss's office. Choose a time when you will not be interrupted.

When you make your presentation, be matter-of-fact, positive, and flexible. Maybe you can settle for less now, in exchange for another raise within the year. Or ask for other benefits, such as extra vacation, more insurance benefits, or more personal days.

End on a positive note. Even if the problem has not been resolved, shake hands and thank your boss for his time and effort. If the first meeting doesn't seem to be productive, set a date to talk again. Don't fence yourself in by delivering an ultimatum.

Be sure to follow up any meeting about money with a memo of understanding: "Just a note to tie up the items we discussed Friday. As I understand it, you agreed to look into my raise by the end of next week. . . ." If there is unreasonable stalling after this, another memo—with copies to Personnel or your boss's boss—may be the answer.

If you fail to get a raise, ask yourself if there is any part of your job you can do better or more quickly to strengthen your case. Are you managing your time well? Could you eliminate duplicated work? Document your improvements and try again in a couple of months.

You may be most effective if you pursue salary increases as part of a group of workers. After all, you probably aren't the only one in your office who is underpaid, and the more people you have behind you, the more your boss will have to listen. For example, you and your coworkers could ask for a general upgrading by showing your boss that employees in your job category deserve to be paid more. Or you could ask for a department-wide raise after completing a difficult project or starting a new office system that improves efficiency. Try building a case for a company-wide adjustment to make up for the undervaluing of women's jobs. Or request an across-the-board cost-of-living increase.

Sandra T., an office worker in a university library, was highly qualified for her job and did it extremely well. Her salary was far below the standard in comparison with other libraries and even within the university itself. But the administration told her that there was just not enough money to go around, and because she believed deeply in the work of the university, she tolerated her low pay for five years. Finally, a coworker approached her with the news that the library employees were forming a union to bargain for higher salaries and negotiate over other issues. At first she was opposed to the idea, but after thinking it over she came to the conclusion that the union might be the only solution to her salary problem. She decided to join and became active in the drive. When the contract was negotiated, it provided for a 10% across-the-board raise plus individual adjustments. Sandra was awarded an extra $2,000.

3.
The Corporate Ladder

You know, the most precious thing about America is
our freedom of choice. I, for instance, chose to be a
bank president. My secretary chose to be a secretary.
—*Tallahassee banker*

The only people who ever hear about job openings in
our department are the supervisor's buddies. If you
don't play softball, you can forget about a promotion,
no matter how qualified you are.
—*Toledo bank clerk*

W HY do women tend to be the "assistants to"? Why
are we so often stuck in dead-end jobs? Why do
we train men to be our superiors?

Both men and women should have access to career
paths if they want them. Women need to break down
some of the doors marked MEN ONLY. At the same time,
however, it is clear that most women will continue to
hold the "women's jobs" that we now occupy. For
many, this will be by choice; for others, by necessity.
Although the corporate ladder exists in every industry,
not everybody gets to climb it. The goal is to maximize
your pay and job satisfaction, no matter what rung you
occupy.

If you're not where you want to be in the working

world, don't make the mistake of thinking that your lack of training or assertiveness alone has put you there. The economy and the structure of the corporate world make it difficult for women to move up, and most women workers are at the bottom of the corporate ladder. A majority of the nation's working women work in a total of only twenty job categories, most of which offer low pay and little advancement opportunity. One working woman in three is an office worker.

While small numbers of women hold nontraditional jobs, the percentage of women working in certain "women's jobs" is increasing. For example, according to the Department of Labor, 86% of all bank tellers were women in 1970. By 1981 that figure had increased to 93%. Few women make it to the top—only 7 out of every 100 working women hold management positions. And this figure has risen by fewer than 3 percentage points in the last twenty years. Office work fits the general

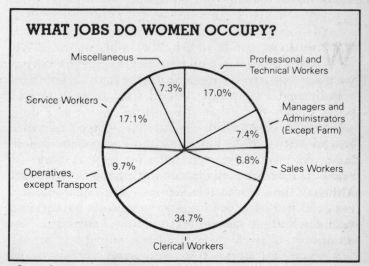

WHAT JOBS DO WOMEN OCCUPY?

Miscellaneous — 7.3%

Professional and Technical Workers — 17.0%

Service Workers — 17.1%

Managers and Administrators (Except Farm) — 7.4%

Operatives, except Transport — 9.7%

Sales Workers — 6.8%

Clerical Workers — 34.7%

Source: Department of Labor, 1982

WHERE ARE THE "WOMEN'S JOBS" IN THE OFFICE?

> fewer than 1% female

Managers earning over $30,000

> 28% female

All Managers and Administrators

> 43% female

Professional and Technical Workers

> 78% female

Clerical Workers

Source: Department of Labor, 1981

pattern, with women heavily represented in the lowest-level jobs and barely present in the higher echelons.

Many of us enter the traditional "women's jobs" by choice, but employers' prejudice and the drive for profits severely restrict our freedom to do otherwise. Patterns of hiring, training, and promotion place enormous obstacles in our career paths. As recently as the 1970s, employment agencies could still be found with color-coded application forms—blue for the men and pink for the women. One agency labeled its professional jobs section "men" and its clerical section "women."

Elizabeth Chang's story is fairly typical. She applied for a job with a major company under the name of E. R. Chang. She didn't hear anything for several weeks, so just to be safe she filed a second, identical resume. She subsequently received two replies. "The one addressed to 'Mr. E. R. Chang' said I had a wonderful background and invited me to call for an interview," she said. "The one addressed to 'Miss E. R. Chang' said I had a good background, but no positions were available."

Many personnel directors might think it odd to hire a

man with a college or graduate degree as a secretary or clerk, but not so with a woman. Men are recruited into positions that pay more and have longer career ladders than the "women's jobs." Many women remain in low-level, low-paying jobs for their entire careers.

A man and his twin sisters joined a major Midwestern insurance company at the same time—the man as a mailroom clerk and the two women as secretaries. The man was quickly tapped for a management training course, while the women were told there were no opportunities to move up. Twelve years later, the man earns twice as much as his sisters.

"It is relatively easy to be promoted to another clerical position," said a Seattle office worker, "but next to impossible to move into one of the many professional positions that open up. Clerical workers are overlooked time and time again."

Clerical workers who want to take courses outside the company to improve their chances for promotion may be denied the tuition reimbursement that is routinely granted to men. For example, a large bank refused to pay one woman for a course in economics on the basis that the course was not "job-related." Six months later, a man in her position was reimbursed for a course in English literature.

Frequently, young male college graduates are hired for middle management or supervisory positions at the expense of older, more experienced women. To add insult to injury, these women are often asked to train the men for their jobs.

One California woman told us that she was hired by a firm as a secretary. But for months, she administered the entire department on her own, while management looked for a "qualified" director. During the next six years, three successive directors—all men—arrived, were trained by her, and then drifted away to other jobs. She was not allowed to apply for paraprofessional positions or even for reclassification. According to the personnel manager, she didn't have the "right kind" of experience.

Career advancement is rarely easy, and it's not for everyone. The following exercises will help you decide on your goals by assessing what in your job gives you satisfaction, enumerating your skills, and rating your chances for mobility at your present company. They should help you decide whether to aim for a promotion, a horizontal move, a raise, or training in a new occupation altogether.

EXERCISE #1:
WHAT IS IMPORTANT TO YOU?
SOURCES OF JOB SATISFACTION

The job characteristics that give people satisfaction are various. Some people place the highest importance on making money; others on helping people. Some like variety; others value predictability.

Read each description of the job factors listed below and decide how important it is to you in your career. Rate the factors using the following scale:

> A—very important to you
> B—somewhat important to you
> C—unimportant or undesirable to you

_____ EXERCISE COMPETENCE: Involve yourself in areas in which you excel.

_____ RESPONSIBILITY: Be responsible for the planning and implementation of many tasks.

_____ PREDICTABILITY: Have a stable work routine and job duties.

_____ HIGH INCOME POSSIBILITIES: Do work that can lead to substantial earnings.

_____ RELATIONSHIPS: Develop close friendships with co-workers.

_____ SECURITY: Be able to depend on keeping your job and making enough money.

_____ ADVANCEMENT: Have the opportunity to move ahead.

_____ CONTACT WITH PEOPLE: Have day-to-day contact with people, deal with the public.

_____ RECOGNITION: Be publicly appreciated and given credit for the quality of your work.

_____ CREATIVITY: Create new programs, systems; formulate new ideas.

_____ SUPERVISION: Direct the work of others.

_____ TIME FREEDOM: Manage your own schedule at work, set your own hours.

_____ LEARNING: Acquire new skills and knowledge.

_____ TEAMWORK: Work with a group toward common goals.

_____ SOCIAL IMPORTANCE: Feel that your work is needed for others' welfare or survival, or to improve society.

_____ PRESSURE: Work against deadlines, receive criticism of your performance.

_____ PERSONAL DEVELOPMENT: Have the opportunity to grow as a person.

_____ LACK OF DEMANDS: Perform duties that require little energy or involvement.

_____ VARIETY: Do a number of different tasks; have work responsibilities change frequently.

_____ DECISION-MAKING: Have the power to decide policies, courses of action.

_____ FUN: Be spontaneous, playful.

_____ ORDERLINESS OF ENVIRONMENT: Work in an environ-

ment where everything has its place and things
rarely change.

_____ INDEPENDENCE: Control the course of your work
without a great deal of direction from others.

_____ STATUS: Have a job which brings respect from
friends, family, and community.

_____ CHALLENGE: Solve problems, test your abilities
frequently.

_____ TRANQUILLITY: Avoid pressures and the "rat race."

_____ SOLITUDE: Work by yourself on projects and tasks.

In Column A below, list the characteristics you coded
as *very important*. In Column B, list those you coded as
somewhat important to you.

A. VERY IMPORTANT	IN YOUR PRESENT JOB	OUTSIDE OF WORK	B. SOMEWHAT IMPORTANT	IN YOUR PRESENT JOB	OUTSIDE OF WORK

Adapted from Howard E. Figler, *PATH: A Career Workbook for Liberal Arts
Students,* Cranston, R.I.: The Carroll Press, 1978.

Now look over your list of *very important* characteristics (Column A). Using the columns provided, check off those that are part of your *present job* and those that are part of your life *outside of work.* Follow the same procedure for Column B.

EXERCISE #2:
WHAT DO YOU DO WELL?
DOES YOUR JOB USE YOUR SKILLS?

Make a list of your skills—both those you use in your present job and those you use or have used outside the job. Did you handle money for a community fund drive? Chances are you can *manage* and *control* funds. Have you been in charge of a church committee? You can *prepare* agendas, *conduct* meetings, and *direct* projects.

Underline those skills that you are using in your present job, and circle those that you are interested in developing further.

Take a careful look at the lists you have made.

• *If neither your present job nor your outside life is providing the satisfactions most important to you,* maybe it is time to think about making a change.
• *If your outside life is far more satisfying than your job life and if you are using few of your skills in your job,* think about whether there are ways to bring your talents into your present job by expanding your duties. Or consider seeking a promotion or looking for a new job that would allow you to exercise your talents for pay.
• *If your job does provide many of the satisfactions that you are looking for and allows you to use many of your best skills,* you may be in the right place. But ask your-

self whether your job description, title, and paycheck adequately reflect your contributions. If not, you may want to ask for a change or to consider a job with another employer who would give you more recognition.

Next, take a close look at your company's policies. Is your employer likely to encourage or to frustrate your career goals? Use the following checklist to determine whether mobility will be relatively easy or difficult at your present or prospective place of employment.

EXERCISE #3: RATE YOUR EMPLOYER

Does the organization implement these policies, which maximize career mobility?

	YES	NO
1. Clear, accurate *job descriptions* for all positions?	☐	☐
2. A consistent system of *job titles*, tied to specific minimum, maximum, and midpoint salary ranges?	☐	☐
3. A policy of *promoting from within*, evidenced by women and minorities holding jobs at many levels?	☐	☐
4. A system of *career paths* that makes it easy for employees to determine which jobs lead where?	☐	☐
5. *Job posting* for all levels of openings in the company, placed where all employees can see them?	☐	☐
6. *On-the-job training* and *career counseling* in varied skills, and not just those limited to clerical work?	☐	☐

7. A policy of recognizing *experience* as well as educational background? □ □

8. Regular *job evaluations* with an opportunity for employee comment? □ □

9. *Tuition reimbursement* for courses at schools and colleges that improve your skills and knowledge? □ □

10. A strong *Affirmative Action Plan* that sets specific goals for hiring, training, and promotion of women and minority employees? (Such plans are required of many firms that do business with goverment.) □ □

If the answer to more than five of these questions is yes, chances are that you can work your way up (or sideways). If the answer to five or more is no, your chances may not be so good.

What should you do if your employer fails the test? You could narrow your career goals to fit your company's limited opportunities. You could look for another job outside the company. Or you could stick it out and try to change your company's policies.

If this last option seems impossible, take heart. With a little ingenuity, you might well be able to persuade your employer to implement new policies that encourage mobility for women.

For example, a woman bank worker sent her boss this memo proposing job posting, a system whereby a company prominently posts information about new job openings within the organization:

Many major companies have initiated the practice of job posting. _____ Bank would benefit by adopting this practice as well.

Job posting would help employees who are immobilized in low-paying, dead-end jobs to move up through the ranks into better-paying positions. It would also give employees the opportunity for lateral moves into areas which they might find more challenging, or offering a higher potential for job advancement.

Job posting is a valuable tool for promoting a good employee/employer relationship. It tells employees that their company is interested in their welfare, progress, and career future. The knowledge that employees have the opportunity to transfer into different departments if they are unhappy or unsuited for their present positions could very well cut down a high turnover rate.

Job posting is a fair employment practice, and one the Bank should initiate.

Not only was her proposal accepted by management but she was awarded a cash prize for her suggestion.

When a group of women brought a similar proposal for job posting to the personnel manager of one New England firm, she turned it down, saying that such a policy would damage employee morale; too many employees would feel rejected when their bids for promotion were unsuccessful. "But my door is always open," she said, by way of offering an alternative. "Call me or drop by whenever you want to know if a job is available." The women took her at her word; all of them called several times a day to ask if any jobs had opened up. After a few days, the personnel manager decided that job posting would do wonders for employee morale.

In a third company, women employees circulated a questionnaire among their coworkers, asking them to describe their interest in company-sponsored career training. They then presented the results and a list of proposals to the personnel office. The company responded by greatly expanding its tuition-reimbursement program.

A union contract can be another effective means of opening up career opportunities. For example, in its contract negotiations, the Service Employees International Union encourages employers to participate in its Lifelong Education and Development (LEAD) program, in which the union and the employer jointly supply training resources for in-company advancement. Some employees are granted time off during the workday to receive the training.

A NOTE ON CAREER TRAINING

Some people are able to look ahead five or ten years and make plans for reaching long-term goals; others think ahead one step at a time. Whatever your time frame, take an active approach to reaching your goal. Investigate how policy changes are made and research job opportunities that might be available to you. Find out what qualifications are necessary for a position you are interested in and determine how you can acquire them.

One cautionary note about career training, however: if you're not sure what you want to do in your present field or in a new field, taking an introductory course at a college, a continuing-education program, or a vocational school might familiarize you with the possibilities and broaden your thinking. But if you hope that this alone will result in a specific career goal such as a job change, promotion, or raise, don't invest your time and money before doing some research.

Ask your boss or personnel officer how taking a particular course will affect your future at the company. You may learn that your company promotes employees on the basis of job performance and seniority rather than educational attainment. And if training is important, it may be on-the-job and in-house training courses, not outside education, that make the greatest difference. Regarding prospective employers, use the Yellow Pages of the telephone book if necessary to find several in your field of interest. Call their personnel offices and ask how the training you are considering would affect your chances of employment and your starting salary.

As for financing your education, many businesses reimburse employees for all or part of the tuition for college courses pursued after work hours. Ask your supervisor or the personnel officer if you are eligible for such a program, and whether the course must pertain to the job you currently have, or whether you can be reimbursed for taking courses that help you advance.

If you do not have access to tuition reimbursement, you may be able to obtain a grant or scholarship from a federal or state government program, or from a college, club, church, or private foundation. Low-interest loans are available through banks, savings and loan associations, and credit unions; payment is usually deferred until after graduation.

Before enrolling in a course, visit several schools to compare costs, financial aid, and course requirements. Find out whether you will have access to an office of career planning or a job-placement service. Ask whether you can receive college credit for past work experience through the College Level Examination Program or other arrangement. Are courses and services offered at convenient times and locations?

As for vocational schools, many make fraudulent claims. Ask how many of the school's graduates have jobs and what their starting salaries were.

Many of us seek to develop our potential at work. But the corporate world places severe limits on how many women can advance and how far we can go. If our feeling of self-worth stems from how high a position we can attain, few of us will feel like valuable employees. We must strive for a far wider range of job satisfactions—fair compensation, the exercise of skills and abilities that give us pleasure, pleasant working relationships, learning how to do something new, advancing a goal we believe in. And the very act of pushing for the mobility and job fulfillment we deserve can provide satisfaction in itself.

4.
Health Hazards
for Office Workers

For a year and a half, I worked three feet from a copier with the exhaust facing me. It got so bad, I felt I was being poisoned. It's important that I have won a workers' compensation claim ... but I cannot place an order for a new pair of lungs and I cannot wipe the worried look from the faces of the members of my family when I can't breathe, I can't stop coughing, and I have to sit up to sleep.

—Pennsylvania secretary

Executives get the best chairs, and secretaries get the worst, which is too bad, because secretaries spend more time in them.

—University professor who designed model chairs

Do you suffer from backaches or headaches? After a few hours of typing, do your neck and shoulders hurt? Are you drowsy by 3:00 P.M. and exhausted by 5:00?

In the past, such ailments were considered minor annoyances and accepted as "just part of the job." Office work, unlike industrial work, was considered safe, clean, and healthful. Today, although the full extent of the health hazards of office work is still unknown, studies have firmly established that the problems can be serious and are widespread. Scientists, medical personnel, and office workers themselves are increasingly worried about the effects on our health of poor office air quality, constant sitting in badly designed chairs, excessive noise, improper lighting, problems associated with new office machines, and job stress.

Furthermore, office job hazards appear to be worsening. The spread of office automation is maximizing the factors that can lead to stress-related disease—factors such as long hours of sitting, machines that cause muscle strain, and endless repetition of monotonous tasks. The drive for energy conservation has led to the "sealing" of older buildings and the construction of "tight" new offices. Inadequate ventilation recycles bacteria, dust, cigarette smoke, and harmful chemicals throughout the building.

No civilized employer would knowingly endanger the health of employees merely to boost profits. But even those who do try to save money by skimping on noise control devices or fresh air supply may be making a financial mistake. Productivity plummets when employees are distracted by discomfort. Uncomfortable chairs, poor air quality, and continual close work lead to a decline in efficiency and accuracy. The mid-afternoon slump may bear a direct relationship to the air quality in the office. And job-related health hazards can result in lost work time. In 9 to 5's survey of over 1,000 office workers in Cleveland and Boston, we found that one in five had missed work because of job-related health problems. A further reason why cost-conscious employers should make the office safe is that increasing numbers of office workers are winning workers' compensation claims for problems arising from stress, exposure to toxic fumes, and disabling back problems.

The solutions to many office health hazards are simple and inexpensive. As the office work force grows, economics and human decency alike demand that these hazards be addressed.

To identify health hazards in your office, begin by asking yourself these questions:

1. Would you rate your overall health as ＿＿ better than ＿＿ the same as ＿＿ worse than it was before you were employed at your present job?
2. Do you experience any of these health problems as a result of your job?
   ＿＿ Eyestrain
   ＿＿ Headaches
   ＿＿ Muscle strain, pain in back or neck or both
   ＿＿ Exhaustion or severe fatigue at day's end
   ＿＿ Digestive/stomach problems
   ＿＿ Pain in arms, shoulders, or both
   ＿＿ Varicose veins
   ＿＿ Insomnia
   ＿＿ Aching wrists or tendons of the hands
   ＿＿ Nausea or dizziness
   ＿＿ Skin rashes or irritation
   ＿＿ Anxiety, depression
   ＿＿ Irritability
3. Have any of these problems caused you to lose time from work? ＿＿ yes ＿＿ no
4. Is your life outside of work negatively affected by your job? ＿＿ yes ＿＿ no

Many office workers who suffer from such health problems may not associate them with their job, may consider them the "normal" effects of a day at the office, or may assume that something is wrong with their bodies, rather than with their office. But every one of these symptoms *can* be caused by problems in the office environment. And every one of them may be relieved by correcting such problems. As you read about the key office health hazards and their solutions, think about your office, how it measures up and how it might be improved. (Health problems can stem from many causes. Consult a physician for diagnosis and treatment for any that concern you.)

OFFICE DESIGN

Good lighting, a quiet environment that allows us to concentrate, and well-designed chairs are vital to the health of those who sit and do close work all day.

Yet some office workers work in areas where lighting is described as twilight, while others suffer from glare. Scientists are raising concerns about the long-term health effects of using fluorescent lighting alone; they recommend that it be combined with full-spectrum light (such as that in a regular light bulb).

If you must strain or squint to see your work, you need better lighting. A combination of diffuse and direct light is ideal. Diffuse background light can be provided by multiple lighting sources, with walls and ceilings serving as reflecting surfaces. A lamp on your desk can supplement this with direct light. Glare can be controlled by shielding light sources (windows should have shades or blinds), using nonreflecting materials and colors, and positioning lighting sources so that they shine on the work, not into the eyes.

If you work continually on a keypunch machine, Addressograph, or tabulating machine in a small, confined room, you are subjected to a potentially hazardous noise level. Noise can cause stress and fatigue, and high noise levels can cause permanent partial hearing loss.

Eight women worked in a bank office filled with such loud word-processing machines that three executives in

the office next door moved because they couldn't stand
the noise. One of the women, who wore a hearing aid,
was bothered by the noise and consulted a doctor, who
told her that such a high level could further damage her
hearing. When her seven coworkers heard this, they
reasoned that their own hearing could also be damaged.
They called the manufacturer of the machines and
learned that inexpensive noise-reducing covers were
available for the printing elements. At their monthly
meeting with their supervisor, they presented a proposal for the purchase of the covers.

Hoping to avoid the expense of the covers, the supervisor decided to call in an inspector from the Occupational Safety and Health Administration for an official
ruling on whether the office was too noisy. The inspector's machine registered the noise level as being within
acceptable government limits, but the inspector's ears
made the same demand that the women were making.
"It's too loud in here," he said. "Buy the covers." The
supervisor complied.

High noise levels are usually avoidable. Carpets,
plants, and walls and ceilings made of porous materials
can lower noise levels, as can mats and inexpensive
plastic shields for typewriters and other machinery.
Noisy equipment should be located as far from other
work areas as possible.

According to a 1979 government survey, as many as
25% of keyboard operators may suffer from occupational cervico-brachial syndrome, a pattern of neck, arm,
shoulder, and back strain. It is estimated that a total of
93 million missed workdays can be attributed to backaches each year.

Rest breaks and job rotation can relieve sitting problems. And merely from a cost-benefit point of view, an
employer should buy every office worker her own chair,
as many occupational health researchers recommend.

YOUR OFFICE CHAIR

An office chair should swivel. The height of the seat and the placement of the backrest should be adjustable. The seat should be upholstered with porous material, and its front rounded off so that it does not cut into the backs of your legs.

To check whether your chair fits you, first stand in front of it. The highest part of the seat should be two inches lower than the crease behind your knees. Now sit down. The lower part of your middle back should touch the backrest while your hips and knees are at right angles to your torso and your feet are flat on the floor. The edge of the seat should be five inches from the crease behind your knees.

If your chair does not fit you, ask your boss to purchase a good one or to help you look for another on the premises. When you find one, put a name tag on it.

If you can't obtain a chair that fits you, try using a pillow on your seat or against the backrest, or try placing a footrest—a phone book will do—under your desk. Also be sure to face your work directly, avoid hunching your shoulders, and move around frequently to ease tight muscles. Stand up and walk around during breaks.

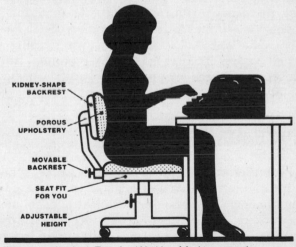

KIDNEY-SHAPE
BACKREST

POROUS
UPHOLSTERY

MOVABLE
BACKREST

SEAT FIT
FOR YOU

ADJUSTABLE
HEIGHT

Illustration by Jack Tom for *Working Mother* magazine

Such a chair is relatively inexpensive and can pay for itself almost immediately, since it eliminates the inefficient, awkward motions necessary in a nonadjustable chair. Dr. E. R. Tichauer, a professor at New York University, estimates that a well-constructed chair can add as much as forty productive minutes to your workday—a total of twenty extra workdays a year.

Accidents, injuries, and fire hazards are further consequences of poor office design. The U.S. Department of Labor estimates an annual rate of 40,000 disabling accidents among the nation's office workers, as well as approximately 200 office-related deaths per year. The most frequent causes are falls and slips, lifting, and unstable file cabinets and shelving. Accidents occur most frequently during or after an office move and during rush periods, when deadlines must be met.

Many office buildings contain serious fire hazards, including overcrowded work areas, wide-open spaces that allow flames and smoke to spread quickly, inadequate emergency exits, and synthetic materials that emit poisonous fumes if they catch on fire. Such hazards can be reduced by clearing passageways, using well-designed equipment that is securely mounted, training employees in emergency procedures, and ensuring that fire safety devices are in working order.

OFFICE AIR QUALITY

Office supplies and machines that emit fumes, synthetic building and furniture materials, and inadequate ventilation systems can pose serious health problems for office workers. The effects of poor office air quality can include fatigue, headaches, eye and throat irritation, nausea, colds, menstrual irregularities, bronchitis, and even long-term respiratory diseases and cancer.

So many outbreaks of building-related health problems have occurred recently that scientists have coined a new term—"tight building syndrome"—to describe the outbreaks of such "mystery illnesses" as large numbers of employees falling asleep at their desks or being overcome with nausea or dizziness. Researchers attribute the phenomenon to the combined effects of air pollutants, an inadequate supply of fresh air, and stressful working conditions.

For a sampling of toxic materials in the office, let's observe Alice H. as she prepares a letter for her boss.

The carbonless typing paper she uses is made with abietic acid and PCBs—polychlorinated byphenyls. While in trace amounts these are not considered major health threats, both can lead to dermatitis and allergic reactions. They cling to hands and fingers and end up in the eyes, where they can cause irritation. In large doses, PCBs can cause severe liver damage and possibly cancer.

Alice goes to make a copy of the letter on the photocopy machine, which may emit ozone, a substance dangerous to the lungs. Such machines are often located in small, windowless rooms or closets to reduce office noise. In these poorly ventilated areas, it's not hard to raise the ozone level to at least twice the federal standard. The black powder in the machine, the toner, may contain highly toxic nitropyrene or trinitrofluorenone.

While in the copying room, Alice breathes in methanol from the duplicating machine, long-term exposure to which can cause liver damage. She ends her hazardous journey by filing the copy of the letter in a plastic file made with polyvinyl chloride, which can cause skin lesions and dermatitis when handled over a long period of time.

As for building materials, many of us work in buildings erected between 1955 and 1970—a boom time for construction—when asbestos was commonly used for fire insulation. That asbestos may now be flaking off and getting into the air circulated by the ventilation system. Inhaling asbestos fibers can cause incurable lung cancer.

Your building may have urea formaldehyde foam insulation, and formaldehyde may be used as a binder in space dividers, shelves, and walls. Formaldehyde typically gives off fumes whose short-term effects can include nausea, dizziness, breathing difficulties, and burning eyes. No one knows what the long-term effects are, but formaldehyde does cause cancer in laboratory rats. The use of urea formaldehyde foam insulation has now been banned in some states.

The problems associated with poisons in the products we use and in the air we breathe are made worse by energy-related money-saving measures such as sealed windows and reduced air circulation. While fifteen to twenty complete changeovers of fresh air per working day are recommended, an "energy-efficient" building might allow only one air exchange every ten hours.

Cigarette smoke in the office environment is a hazard to smokers and nonsmokers alike. According to one environmental consultant, "The level of particulate matter in office buildings where smoking is allowed is ten to one hundred times higher than the allowable limits for outside air." Where smoking is permitted, five times the normal ventilation is required to remove the toxic chemicals released.

The proliferation of toxic materials in the office is alarming. Fortunately, many of the problems caused by poor office air quality are easy and inexpensive to correct. If a stuffy office is troubling you, check to see whether there are any "dead spaces" in your vicinity— areas in which no air is replaced and in which pollutants can build up. You can test for dead spaces by lighting a match or cigarette and watching to see if the smoke moves out of the area. If it hangs in the air for minutes, airborne pollutants probably do too.

Problems with ventilation can be dealt with by regularly cleaning the ventilation system, ensuring that no vents are blocked by file cabinets or partitions, and keeping the system on for more hours of the day. (To check whether the system is turned on, hold a tissue near a vent; if it moves, air is circulating.) In addition, photocopiers and other printing machines should be placed in a well-ventilated room, away from desks. They should have exhaust vents.

To assess the hazards in office supplies such as typewriter correction fluid, write to the manufacturer for a "material data safety sheet." Safer substitutes can often be found for hazardous products. If not, your employer should provide you with protective gloves where appropriate (for example, for the employee who must handle photocopier toner). Avoid inhalation as much as possible and wash your hands immediately after using the substance.

OFFICE MACHINES

Of the various kinds of new office equipment, the video-display terminal (VDT) is the most common. The video-display terminal (or "CRT," for the cathode-ray tube inside) features a televisionlike screen that displays information stored by a computer. The long-term health effects of years of sitting before a flickering screen for eight hours a day have not yet been determined, but the short-term effects are already clear, the most common complaints being eyestrain, neck and back pain, headaches, blurred vision, and mood changes such as irritability and depression.

A 1981 study by the National Institute for Occupational Safety and Health (NIOSH) found that clerical workers working full-time on VDTs had higher stress ratings than any other group of workers the agency had studied, including air-traffic controllers.

Scientists are concerned that full-time VDT use may be linked to the development of cataracts. They are also alarmed by the higher than average rates of adverse pregnancies—miscarriages and babies born with birth defects—afflicting groups of VDT users in the United States and Canada. Very low levels of radiation emitted by the tubes in the machines, the possible emission of chemical fumes, and the stressful pace of VDT work have all been suggested as causes.

Each and every one of these problems is relatively easy to solve. In fact, a writer for a management research firm notes that protections against VDT operator discomfort "are to a great extent within the control of the office manager."

The terminal itself should adjust to the worker, not vice versa. The height and tilt of the screen should be adjustable so that the employee can view the screen with her eyes looking slightly downward. A detachable keyboard is ideal, as it allows the employee to sit comfortably rather than straining to reach the keyboard and see the screen at the same time. The screen should be made of nonreflecting glass, and the brightness of the letters should be adjustable. Other remedies for glare include shades or blinds on windows, dimmer lighting, an antiglare shield, and nonreflective surfaces surrounding the machine. Regular eye exams and special work glasses can also reduce eyestrain problems.

Metal shielding that significantly reduces the emission of radiation by VDTs can be provided by the manufacturer for a fraction of the machine's cost. In addition, a Canadian government task force has recommended that pregnant women be allowed to transfer to other work tasks—with no loss of pay—during their pregnancy, and that no one work on a VDT for more than five hours a day.

To reduce eyestrain and stress, VDT operators should take rest breaks away from their machines. NIOSH recommends a fifteen-minute break every two hours, and fifteen minutes per hour for operators working under heavy pressure. Other work can be done during these breaks; the important thing is to give the eyes an opportunity to look at greater distances. Another remedy is to alternate two hours of screen work with two hours of another kind of work, which should involve focusing on greater distances and moving the body.

Four typesetters operating VDTs at an advertising agency found to their dismay that eyestrain made them unable to read at night after work. They asked their boss if a 9 to 5 member who had studied office health and safety could inspect the office and make suggestions for change. He agreed. The "inspector" recommended purchasing a window shade and moving two of the typesetters so that they no longer faced the window. She suggested glare shields and clip-on lamps for the typesetting equipment and the removal of some of the fluorescent tubing from the overhead lights. The employer implemented all of these suggestions, solving the typesetters' eyestrain problems.

STRESS

The stress response is the body's normal way of preparing to meet a physical, emotional, or mental challenge. A brief stressful event such as a scolding by a supervisor causes short-lived physical changes: faster heartbeat

and breathing, tightening of the stomach, dry mouth.
The body regains its equilibrium quickly after meeting
such a challenge. But if chronic or prolonged stress
keeps the body off balance over a period of weeks or
months, then symptoms of stress can develop, including
insomnia, headaches, backaches, stomachaches, pain in
the neck and shoulders, menstrual irregularity, diar-
rhea, and loss of appetite. And over a period of years,
stress may lead to serious illnesses such as asthma,
ulcers, colitis, hypertension, and coronary heart disease.

Research is beginning to uncover a virtual epidemic
of stress symptoms and stress-related diseases among
office workers. Millions of workers are affected. And
because the symptoms do not disappear at the end of
the workday, millions of families may suffer from the
problems caused by stress in the office.

A 1975 study by NIOSH found that secretaries had the
second highest incidence of stress-related diseases
among workers in 130 occupations. And results from the
Framingham Heart Study (1980) showed that women
office workers developed coronary heart disease at almost twice the rate of other women workers. The eight-
year study found that "economic stress" (lack of money)
was an important predictor of the development of the
disease. These findings helped to put in perspective the
old myth of the beleaguered boss suffering ulcers and
risking a heart attack for his $88,000 job. It may well be
that his secretary runs a higher risk of heart disease,
ulcers, and hypertension, as well as fatigue, depression,
anxiety, and nervousness.

Further research has confirmed that the most stressful jobs are those that involve a combination of high
pressure for output and little control over how the work
gets done. An executive preparing a report for the annual meeting may be working under stress but perhaps not
as much stress as the woman who must finish typing the

report by the end of the day. While the executive has some control over the pace and quality of his work and can call upon assistants, the typist has no such choices.

In 9 to 5's Office-Worker Health and Safety Survey (1980), 70% of the respondents reported "somewhat stressful" or "very stressful" working conditions. The harmful effects of job stress usually result from the cumulative combined effects of a set of job pressures and problems rather than from a single cause. The Health and Safety Survey, reprinted on page 83, reports the top sources of stress.

Your response to stressful conditions could either help you rebound quickly from a stressful situation or heighten the crisis. Take the stress test to evaluate how you deal with job pressures.

When your job makes you angry, frustrated, or annoyed, how often are you likely to:

	NEVER 1	SOME-TIMES 2	OFTEN 3	ALMOST ALWAYS 4
1. Drink alcohol, smoke, use drugs, or take medication	☐	☐	☐	☐
2. Drink more coffee or soda, eat more often	☐	☐	☐	☐
3. Act as though nothing much had happened	☐	☐	☐	☐
4. Keep it to yourself	☐	☐	☐	☐
5. Apologize even though you were right	☐	☐	☐	☐
6. Take it out on others, blame someone else	☐	☐	☐	☐
7. Exercise, walk, jog, dance, meditate, or engage in a hobby	☐	☐	☐	☐
8. Take time off to get away from it all	☐	☐	☐	☐

9. Get it off your chest, blow off steam ☐ ☐ ☐ ☐
10. Talk to a friend or relative as soon ☐ ☐ ☐ ☐
    as you can
11. Take action to prevent the same ☐ ☐ ☐ ☐
    situation from happening again
12. Get people together at work or join ☐ ☐ ☐ ☐
    a group or organization to obtain
    needed changes

If you usually deal with stress by using the methods in questions 1 through 6, you need to learn to change your ways. If, on the other hand, you often or almost always use the methods in questions 7 through 12, you are probably handling job stress in a constructive way.

First you must understand that stress has recognized external causes and can lead to serious medical conditions. It's not just a state of mind, and its source is most likely in your office, not in your head.

Learning to relax for brief periods during the workday and on your way home can help your mind and body deal with stress on the job. One exercise that is commonly recommended is this: close your eyes and pretend that you are being carried away to a relaxing spot. Breathe deeply and imagine lying on a hot, sunny beach or sitting by a still, green pond. Visualize the scene in detail. To end the exercise, take a deep breath, open your eyes, and come back refreshed.

The muscle aches that are common to office workers can be relieved if you take care to do short, simple exercises frequently throughout the day. For head, neck, and shoulder aches, for example, slowly rotate your shoulders, separately and together. Roll your head in a slow circle. Massage your scalp with your fingertips. Stretch your arms over your head; then bend over gently, letting your head and arms hang toward your feet;

OFFICE-WORKER HEALTH AND SAFETY SURVEY

RANK ORDER	SOURCES OF STRESS ON THE JOB	% OF RESPONDENTS
# 1	Lack of promotions or raises	51.7%
# 2	Low pay	49.0%
# 3	Monotonous, repetitive work	40.0%
# 4	No input into decision-making	35.1%
# 5	Heavy work load/overtime	31.5%
# 6	Supervision problems	30.6%
# 7	Unclear job descriptions	30.2%
# 8	Unsupportive boss	28.1%
# 9	Inability or reluctance to express frustration or anger	22.8%
#10	Production quotas	22.4%
#11	Difficulty juggling home/family responsibilities	12.8%
#12	Inadequate breaks	12.6%
#13	Sexual harassment	5.6%

Note: The survey was distributed in Cleveland and Boston in the fall of 1980; 915 respondents answered the questions on stress.

come up slowly. These are only suggestions—do what feels good.

Diet can also have a significant effect on your response to a stressful day at the office. A substantial breakfast high in protein and starch (eggs, milk products, cereal) and a light lunch followed by a brisk walk will maximize your physical resources for the day. During breaks, avoid caffeine and sugar, both of which can increase irritability and make you feel worse, not better. And of course smoking and excessive drinking can cause serious health problems on top of the ones you may already be dealing with.

Exercise or an absorbing hobby can also help to relieve job stress. Use the "substitution principle" cited by Robert L. Veninga and James P. Spradley in their book, *The Work-Stress Connection.* You can relieve your *mental* stress by putting your body under *physical* stress with such activities as swimming, walking, jogging, or playing a competitive sport. If you spent your workday trying to untangle a complicated filing system, don't go home and do a difficult jigsaw puzzle. On the other hand, if you've been under emotional stress—for example, if you handle calls from irate customers whose problems you cannot solve—a mental challenge like a jigsaw puzzle might be just the thing to help you escape.

Recognize the control you could have over your workday and take steps to exercise it. If you have any leeway in how you manage your time at work, use it. A small step such as deciding to handle all the correspondence in one chunk each morning can make a big difference in how you feel about the rest of the day. And make an effort to pamper yourself after a stressful period. Promise yourself a hot bath after a terrible day, or, if you can, a day off after two weeks of rush-season overtime.

Keep in mind that an unsupportive boss may be hazardous to your health, and try to develop friendly and supportive relationships with at least some of your co-workers. And don't keep your anger bottled up. You may not be able to yell back at a boss, but get things off your chest by talking to a coworker. She is probably angry about the same things herself, and together you may think of ways to change some problem situations. If you can't talk to a coworker, at least talk to a friend or relative as soon as possible.

As helpful as diet, exercise, and blowing off steam may be, the only real solution is prevention—eliminating the sources of stress and other office health problems. This means changing the office *environment* by reducing noise, improving ventilation and lighting, and reducing exposure to toxic chemicals. It means changing the *job design* to allow more variety, rest periods, and opportunities to learn new skills and increase employee control over pace and work load. It means improving *employer-employee relations* by providing respect and recognition for employee contributions, establishing grievance procedures, and providing equal opportunity. And it means altering the *corporate policies* that put pressure on working women, by responding to the needs of the working family, supporting continuing education, and improving pay, job security, and access to advancement.

You will probably find that your job-related health problems are not unique to you and that they may not lend themselves to an individual solution. Organizing, whether in the form of a small support group or a union, may be your best bet. Not only do you stand a better chance of changing your working conditions if you use the power of numbers, but the very act of being part of a group can reduce stress.

The first step is to identify the possible sources of health problems in your office. Fill out the Office-Worker Health and Safety Questionnaire.

OFFICE-WORKER HEALTH AND SAFETY QUESTIONNAIRE

OFFICE DESIGN

Is the lighting too dim ☐ too bright ☐
Is your office too noisy ☐
Does your chair cause discomfort or pain ☐
Are there safety or fire hazards in your office ☐

OFFICE AIR QUALITY

Is your office too hot ☐ too cold ☐
Is the supply of fresh air inadequate ☐
Are there irritating fumes in the air ☐
  If so, where do they come from_____

OFFICE MACHINES

If you work with any office machines (video-display terminal, photocopier, and so on), do you experience:
muscle aches or strains ☐
eyestrain ☐
problems with fumes ☐
concern over possible danger during pregnancy ☐

STRESS

Do you have problems with the following potential sources of stress?

Job Design

rapid work pace ☐
high production quotas ☐
constant sitting ☐
lack of variety ☐
underutilization of your skills ☐
responsibility without authority to make decisions ☐
lack of input into how job is done ☐

Employer-Employee Relations

lack of respect or recognition ☐
nonsupportive boss ☐

unclear job description	☐
too many bosses	☐
ineffective or nonexistent grievance procedures	☐
sexual harassment	☐

Corporate Policies

low pay	☐
dead-end job	☐
difficulty balancing work schedule with home/family responsibilities	☐
sex, race, age discrimination	☐
job insecurity	☐

Next, find out whether other employees are bothered by the problems that bother you. You may want to ask some of your coworkers to fill out the questionnaire themselves and return it to you for compilation, or have everyone get together at lunch or after work to discuss the questionnaire together.

If possible, come up with recommendations for solutions. Imagine what you would do if you had the power to correct the problems and create a pleasant, non-stressful work environment in your office. Would you allow typists to get up more frequently to stretch their muscles? Would you move the photocopying machine into a room of its own? What would become of your overbearing supervisor? You may want to gather more information by talking to employees in other departments or by asking questions of your supervisor or building superintendent. Your case will be strengthened if you can spell out how management will benefit from the correction of the problems. In addition to pointing out that healthful working conditions boost productivity, you may want to remind your boss that he inhales the same poisons you do and suffers fatigue from the same stuffy air.

You are now prepared to meet—preferably as a group—with your supervisor or boss. If you have trouble figuring out who in management has jurisdiction over the lights, the chairs, or the ventilation system, start with whoever is closest at hand. Get his or her support for an appeal to whoever is in charge.

If office hazards are affecting your health, you will probably have to pursue a dual approach to making yourself healthier and more comfortable. You may need to change your own behavior (drinking less coffee, for example, or pursuing a relaxing hobby outside of work). And you'll need to effect changes in your work environment to get at the root causes of your health problems. The results should enhance your well-being both in and out of the office.

5.
Automation in the Office

Put yourself in my shoes. Imagine yourself viewing a jet-black screen displaying hordes of small, difficult-to-read, bright green numbers, keeping in mind that you must get these numbers absolutely accurate. You sit in front of this screen for six or seven hours on the night shift without any break, and handle an average of six critical deadlines each night, with your boss at your back.

—Midwestern bank employee

People will adapt nicely to office automation if their arms are broken. We're in the twisting stage now.
—William Laughlin, former vice-president of IBM,
in Business Week, *June 30, 1975*

THE American work force is undergoing enormous changes as clerical work replaces manufacturing employment as the base of the economy. And now clerical work itself is being transformed by automation of the office.

Office automation consists of two basic features: the introduction of new technology and the reorganization of work, or rationalization.

The key element of the new office technology is the word processor, a typewriter with a "memory," whose

OFFICE AUTOMATION GLOSSARY

Computerization: The application of computers to office tasks or procedures.

Microprocessor: A complete computer smaller than a postage stamp, also called a "microcomputer" or "minicomputer." Microprocessors make it possible to use computers economically for very complex purposes.

Rationalization: Breaking work into its smallest parts, taking out the element of decision-making. Each person does a standardized fragment of the larger task. Work becomes routine and repetitive. Also called "routinization" or "scientific management."

Video-Display Terminal (VDT): The key unit of the automated office, used to process text or data, and linked to the computer system. Also called a CRT, referring to the cathode-ray tube around which it is built.

Word Processing: Preparation, editing, storage, and retrieval of text. Takes its place alongside *data processing*—the manipulation of numbers and symbols. Can be done on equipment that stands alone or is connected to a computer-based system.

core is the microprocessor, or computer-on-a-chip, a complete computer made on a tiny silicon chip the size of your fingernail. A word processor is equipped with a video-display terminal (VDT), featuring a typewriterlike keyboard with a televisionlike screen, both wired to a computer base. Whatever the operator types appears on the screen and can be easily corrected. When she is satisfied with her copy, the computer can print out a paper version.

The impact of microprocessors has been compared to that of virtually every major invention in history—the printing press, the cotton gin, the telephone, the steam engine, and atomic energy. The day is not far off when the great majority of jobs will involve the use of computers.

As the largest and fastest-growing sector of the work force, clerical workers will be the most affected by office automation. Computer experts are thinking about you and the place you will occupy in the office of the future. It's time to give some thought to the matter yourself.

What does the office of the future look like? Cockpit-like units with desktop terminals replace your desk and typing stand and even your boss's desk. File cabinets and "in" and "out" boxes are nowhere in sight. Inter-office memos, letters, reports, and budgets formerly recorded on paper are composed, edited, and filed by computer terminals. Documents are sent by "electronic mail" across the country or around the world in a matter of minutes. Meetings and phone calls are replaced by video conferences.

Computer-industry spokesmen talk of advances that seem unbelievable today. Some say that desktop video-display screens will speak and respond to verbal commands within the decade. "By 2038, computers will be alive," predicts one particularly ardent enthusiast, "equipped with IQ's equivalent to the requirements of construction workers or bank tellers."

That may be going too far, but there is no doubt that the changes will be enormous. And automation can have advantages for office workers. A computer system can eliminate tedious clerical work. For example, in law firms it is estimated that a court document is retyped an average of six times on conventional typewriters. With a word processor, which edits texts, the full document need be typed only once, with corrections keyed in as the draft is revised.

One woman who works with electronic communication and text-editing equipment writes, "These are truly marvelous features. In fact, I wouldn't want to do without them now that I have them; they make my working life so much richer and more fun."

Yet many of us are uneasy about the advent of the computer age. Some office workers feel anxious because of a lack of familiarity with machines, or they worry that they don't understand math well enough. One woman told us she lived in fear after hearing that a coworker had pushed the wrong buttons and wiped out the entire New Jersey mailing list for a major magazine. If this "high-tech anxiety" is your problem, you might want to ask your employer if he will pay for you to take an introductory computer science course at a local community college.

But many of the fears go deeper. Though automation offers opportunities, it also harbors serious dangers: the proliferation of dead-end jobs, the displacement of workers by machines, the social isolation of machine operators, and the health problems associated with video-display terminals. It's rational to fear these trends. And some women have turned their concerns into resistance. In fact, employee resistance—not technical problems—is considered the chief obstacle along the path to the fully automated office. And the resistance occurs at all levels, from clerical workers on up.

One woman who was asked to write down all her bookkeeping procedures so her job could be computerized held back some information: "I'm not going to tell them everything just so they can get rid of me," she explained. In 1978, 500 secretaries at the United Nations successfully went on strike for a week when their office was automated without warning. A great many employees express their objections to automation by quitting. A researcher for one of the leading computer-marketing firms told us that "word processing was an initial disaster and still has a 100% annual turnover rate."

Many of us feel threatened because we *are* threatened.

John J. Connell, executive director of the Office Technology Research Group, is concerned that the needs of employees may be overlooked in the rush to automate. "The heavy emphasis is on the equipment and its implications for productivity and efficiency," he says. "Minimal consideration has been given thus far to the impact on people."

Unless more consideration is given to the impact on people, the office of the future is going to look very much like the factory of the past. Like the pieceworkers of earlier days, VDT operators are sometimes paid for each item they produce—in this case, the number of lines they process. Automated offices often switch to factorylike shift work to keep their expensive machines busy day and night. And there is a small but growing trend toward "office homework." Doing a computer job in your home may not be much different from running a sewing machine in the kitchen in turn-of-the-century New York.

Office technology itself is neither good nor bad. Machines can be directed to do just about anything you want them to do. In shaping the office of the future, our employers will continue to ignore our best interests in favor of their own interests as long as we let them. We must be aware of some of the problems of automation and turn them into opportunities. It's time we turned our resistance into action for change.

THE PROBLEMS

1. Pay

While office technology creates opportunities for higher pay for some of us, for many others it is used as an excuse for keeping salary levels down. An employer may ignore the new skills you have learned in order to operate your machine and argue that it's the machine itself that does all the work so that *you* are worth less. Numerous studies cited at a 1978 European conference on computers and work show that secretarial output can increase from 25% to 150% when word-processing equipment is used. But the pay may not increase by one penny. In some cities, VDT operators earn less than conventional typists despite their higher skill and productivity.

If your productivity goes up dramatically—particularly if you've learned new skills or have adapted to difficult working conditions—you should be compensated by an increase in pay, more break time (for health reasons as well), a reduction in hours without a reduction in pay, or a combination of all of these.

2. Job Design

Many women are drawn to secretarial and office work because it is service-oriented and varied while offering opportunities for contact with people. High on the list of things we appreciate about our work are a natural work pace, the opportunity to exercise judgment, and recognition for work performed. And these are the very features most threatened by automation.

Most managers believe that efficient office automation involves close supervision of clerical workers who perform particular tasks on equipment designed to maximize high volume and speed. Carol F.'s job as a computer-terminal operator is a good example: "I worked for seven and a half hours a day typing the letters and numbers off the top line of a green form into the terminal. As soon as I finished one, I turned to the next form, and the next, and the next. The letters didn't even make any sense. You don't have to be a college graduate to hate that kind of work."

Computer technology makes it possible to break jobs down into very small tasks and to keep close track of how quickly employees complete those duties—by the day, by the hour, and even by the minute. In a company in which employees handle phone calls from customers, a computer can measure the average delay in answering calls, the amount of time used to process each call, and the number of calls each clerk handles per day. A video-display terminal can record the number of keystrokes per minute and the number of lines processed per day. And one major insurance company measures the output of its office workers in $6\frac{1}{2}$-minute units—almost 74 measurements a day! "That machine feels like a foreman breathing down my neck," one woman complained.

It is not only irritating to work under these conditions—it's not very good for productivity either. For example, North Carolina State University researcher B. H. Beith finds that machine monitoring and machine pacing (with items appearing on the screen at a set speed that you have to keep up with) tend to *reduce* productivity. When phone company employees persuaded management to stop monitoring their calls, productivity *went up*. And the less control you have over the pace of your work and the more you are monitored by machine, the more mistakes you make. The error rate can increase by anywhere from 40% to 400%.

Rationalization—breaking down tasks into their smallest parts—can also be counterproductive. A bank redesigned a certain job so that all the employees did all day was type numbers onto forms. To their dismay, the managers found that the error rate soared so high that they had to hire an equal number of "checkers" to correct the errors.

It makes sense, doesn't it? You work faster, more productively, and more accurately when you are satisfied and challenged by your work. If you find your job stressful and boring, it's more difficult to do it well. If your employer chooses to rationalize, monitor, and machine-pace your job, he may achieve greater control over your work, but at a heavy cost to you and to the company.

3. Computer Career Ladders for Women?

The accompanying chart, Growth of Computer Jobs by 1990, shows how the major types of computer jobs will grow over the next seven years. There will be millions of new jobs in the coming decades, and as women we should have as big a piece of the high-level jobs as of the low-level. But so far the signs are not encouraging. To date, 78% of the women employed in the computer field occupy the lowest-level jobs, according to the Department of Labor. (Women make up 95.6% of keypunch operators, 75% of all office-machine operators, and 62% of computer operators.) A sociological study of five large employers in 1977 found that when computerization was introduced, clericals were rarely upgraded to fill new skilled jobs. The main avenues for clerical workers were either horizontal or downward.

The new jobs opening up in the computer field could provide the key to a new era of pay equity. If we could move freely into the computer jobs we are qualified for, the old patterns of discrimination and low-paying "women's jobs" could be broken.

GROWTH OF COMPUTER JOBS BY 1990

NAME OF JOB	JOB DESCRIPTION	PROJECTED GROWTH
Data-entry employees	Feed information into computer	– 3.0%*
Word-processing operators	Run electronic typewriters with computer memories	+76.8%
Programmers	Write instructions telling the computer what to do	+60.5%
Systems analysts	Design best use of the computer at any given moment	+78.6%
Computer maintenance employees	Keep computer in good repair	+104.0%

*Data-entry employees—particularly keypunch operators—will be less in demand as electronic equipment makes it possible for a variety of workers to enter information directly into the computer.

Source: U.S. Department of Labor

4. Job Loss and Decline of Skilled Jobs

The purpose of automation is to do more work with fewer people. So far, however, the clerical industries are growing so fast that automation has not cut down on the total number of clerical jobs. For example, a bank may reduce its check-processing work force by fifteen workers by introducing automation. But at the same time it may expand its credit-card operation, creating a need for twenty new workers in that department. The demand for office workers is still high and still increasing.

But that demand is not as high as it would be if there were no new machines, and it is not increasing as fast. At some point there may not be any new clerical jobs available for workers whose jobs have been phased out by automation. Researchers in France and Great Britain are already worried about potential massive clerical unemployment in their countries. The same thing could happen here.

Further, while the number of jobs has not been a problem so far, the *nature* of the jobs eventually could be. While some administrators are trying to use new technology to improve clerical jobs, many more prefer to create "deskilled" jobs in an effort to keep clerical wages as low as possible. Trained and experienced employees may face the no-win proposition of employment in a deskilled position or no employment at all.

When automated equipment was introduced in an airline office, women with seventeen years of seniority were downgraded to the point where they were working at almost entry-level jobs. Frightened middle managers took over routine office duties in an attempt to save their own jobs.

In some offices, the advent of word processing means

that individual bosses no longer have their own secretaries. Dorothy N. told us: "When automation came to my office, all secretarial positions were abolished. Some of the secretaries went into the typing pool as typists. The rest, including me, became clerks. I spend about one hundred percent of my time filing and running errands for seven people."

5. Health Hazards

There are two general areas of concern regarding health in the automated office. The first is the rash of problems related directly to the machines themselves: eyestrain from poor lighting and problems in the video-display screens; back and muscle strain from improperly designed work stations and chairs; and stomach and breathing problems from chemical emissions.

The second area is a host of stress-related diseases stemming from the pressures of low-paid, fast-paced, repetitive jobs over which we have little decision-making power. Stress is fast becoming the characteristic occupational hazard of the computer age.

Surely the inventiveness that led to the development of the silicon chip can also be used to create interesting, safe jobs.

WHEN AUTOMATION COMES IN

"When my company decided to automate," says Juanita D., "my supervisor and I went shopping for word processors together. The salesmen said to me, 'If you're bright, as you obviously are, you can do a tremendous amount of work on this machine and produce spectacular results.' Then they took my supervisor aside and confided, 'A moron can be fully functional in three hours.' "

Managers who want to introduce automation as effectively as possible are advised to make sure it improves the jobs of current employees in addition to boosting efficiency. Some employers follow this advice and consult their employees before automating the office, but often the changes are made first and announced later.

Be warned that automation may be on the way if you are asked to fill out a questionnaire describing your job functions, if efficiency experts arrive and begin setting up new procedures, or if your job is simplified. The sooner you find out about the changes to come, the greater the chance that you will have some influence regarding them.

Kathy K., a secretary at a university, was alarmed when she heard that management wanted to bring in word-processing equipment. She and the other women in her department decided to conduct their own investigation of computer equipment and make recommendations to management. Their boss was impressed with their information and convinced by their argument that the secretaries' concerns were vital to the success of automating the office. When it came time to purchase the equipment, three secretaries, a computer programmer from the central office, and a professor from the department surveyed the options and made the decisions as a team. The secretaries also insisted that they all learn to use the new equipment; in that way they prevented one or two secretaries' having exclusive access to the machines and thereby full-time jobs as word processors.

You can take steps to make sure the best features of office automation are implemented, if your employer is open-minded and if you are willing to push him in the right direction. You might use the following questions to begin a dialogue in which you can voice preferences concerning your job description and the use of the machines.

- What will my duties be? Will I be involved in the completion of a whole task, or will I merely enter data into a machine?
- Will I be trained to use new skills?
- Will I work for one person or more than one? Will I be seated in a separate word-processing center? Who will supervise me?
- Will I have control over the pace and organization of my work? Or will the pace of my work be set by the machine? Will the machine monitor my output?
- Will I receive a higher salary for learning new job skills?

TRAINING FOR COMPUTER CAREERS

The *Occupational Outlook Handbook*, published by the U.S. Department of Labor and available at your local library, describes the jobs, their requirements, and the opportunities that will be opening up within the decade. Generally, for jobs in data entry, operations, manufacturing, and administrative support, you will need only a high school diploma or its equivalent. A college education is usually but not always required of programmers, systems analysts, sales personnel, computer design workers, and managers.

For all computer occupations, employers stress the importance of on-the-job training. In an ideal in-house training program, anyone who wants to learn how to use the equipment should have the opportunity. And you should be able to make use of a broad range of the equipment's powers. (Some managers program the machines to perform only a fraction of what they are capable of—or train the employees in only a few uses.) Further, clericals should have the opportunity to be trained for the "good" computer jobs that are created, such as data-base management and computer programming.

Set out to educate yourself about the full capacity of the computer system in your office, and talk to your boss about it. You might try these methods of learning more about how the new equipment works:

- Take a course at a community college. (Make sure that the course covers the type of equipment used in your office.)
- Ask to work with the training manual (if there is one) on your own, or have your supervisor train you and some coworkers.
- Ask your boss if he will block out some time each week for you to experiment with the machine. You may be able to design new ways to do your job faster and better.
- If your computer is programmed to do only a few specific tasks, tell your boss you are interested in doing more with it. Suggest some ways that the computer could save you time.

If we were to draw up a Technology Bill of Rights for the office of the future, it might read like this:

We use more skills, not fewer.
We have more control over the pace and organization
of the work, not less.
We can exercise more judgment, not less.
We are protected from health hazards.

We are trained in the use of the system.
We participate in the design of the system.
We are compensated for our higher productivity.
We share in the benefits of technology.

Redirecting the course of office automation to ensure that these provisions are made may seem impossible. Some people in management think that such a vision of the ideal office of the future is hopelessly unrealistic. But while the United States leads the way in technological advances, Europeans are taking the lead in the intelligent use of the new machines. As a result, the well-being and professionalism of European office workers are far better protected than our own, and we would do well to learn from their example.

In Norway the Worker's Environment Act calls for an end to monotonous work. It recommends that the professional development of the employees be considered in the designing of jobs and mandates that employees— not machines—set the pace of work. In some European countries, rest breaks after every few hours of work on a VDT are required. Union agreements in Austria limit continuous work on a VDT to four hours a day. And "new technology agreements" throughout Europe require that unionized employees be both notified in advance of technological changes and retrained if their current jobs will be eliminated.

We can't stop automation, and we wouldn't necessarily want to. But we can attempt to use the machines in such a way that they result in a better way of life for all of us rather than causing more problems. Fortunately, office automation is still in the process of development. We have the opportunity to shape its use so that it satisfies our employers' desire for higher productivity at the same time that it promotes our own sense of well-being and job satisfaction.

6.
Issues for the Working Family

I asked to use my vacation time when my son was in the hospital with appendicitis. My boss flew into a rage and said, "If your family is more important to you than your job, you're not the right person for this company."

—Minneapolis secretary

My company runs as if every employee has a wife at home to look after the kids and cook dinner. But in my house, I'm the employee *and* the wife.

—Miami word-processing operator

OLD myths die hard. The stereotype of the man who goes off to work and brings home the bacon to his homemaker wife and their children presently applies to only 12% of all American families. Yet when we hear "normal family," that's still what comes to mind.

Not only do many of us hold on to inappropriate images of modern family life, we also think that they prevailed throughout Western history. They didn't. The so-called traditional family has had a relatively short life span. Before industrial times, the family was the primary economic unit, and both men and women contributed to the financial welfare of the household. It was only when factories, not farms and villages, became the site of production that the division of men's and women's roles became rigid and distinct: the husband provided the income and the wife took care of home and family.

Even while this model was developing, though, many women worked outside the home in mills and factories and as domestic servants. By the 1920s, one in five American women was working; by the 1940s, one in three. And though women returned to the home after World War II, they were soon back in the work force; by the mid-1950s, their employment levels approached the wartime high.

In the 1970s and 1980s, the continuing trend has been marked by a dramatic new phenomenon—the massive entry of mothers of young children into the work force. Most American children now grow up in families in which the mothers work outside the home.

Why are mothers working today? Many because they want to, most because they must. For increasing numbers of two-parent families, it is no longer possible to subsist on one income alone; a second income is the difference between poverty and economic security. And one family in six is headed by a single woman.

When mothers began to work outside the home in large numbers, social scientists issued dire warnings about the damaging effects a mother's job would have on her child's development. Millions of women went to work each day feeling guilty. Then came new studies, by researcher Alison Clarke-Stewart and others, which said that children's development was not harmed by their mothers' employment. In some cases, in fact, children in day-care centers developed faster and better than children at home with their mothers. Don't feel guilty, researchers told us; it's okay to go to work. And they were right. We shouldn't feel guilty, but we should feel angry.

We live in a society that upholds the image of the full-time mother while at the same time making it difficult for a family to live on one income. We work in a business world that expects us and our children to do all the adjusting to rigid company policies. And we must make do with a child-care system that is often inadequate and costly.

To this day, the work world continues to operate as if mothers stayed at home and fathers went off to work. The enormous burdens on the family are not often recognized. Indeed, the very existence of the family is often ignored.

Observing the throngs of workers clogging the streets during the morning rush hour, you might be hard-pressed to remember that their children existed at all. Yet every weekday, millions of children with working parents are too sick to go to the babysitter's. On a school holiday, 23½ million children may be home on vacation, necessitating complicated babysitting arrangements. But no matter what is happening with their children, working mothers are expected to sit down promptly each morning at their typewriters, looking fresh and trim, and to devote themselves to the work before them with wholehearted concentration.

CORPORATE POLICIES

It would be easier to run a household and hold down a job at the same time if employers were more willing to recognize the special needs of working mothers and to alter corporate policies accordingly. Nor would the mothers be the only ones to benefit from such a change: many studies have shown that programs that aid the working parent aid the employer as well.

A dramatic example is reported by Alice Duncan, director of a child-care center serving children of employees at Intermedics in Freeport, Texas. Reduced absenteeism and a lessened turnover rate resulted in savings to the company of more than $2 million in the first two years of operation of the child-care program. A 1979 survey conducted by the University of Wisconsin of fifty-eight organizations that sponsored some form of child care showed 57% of these companies reporting lower job turnover, 72% reporting lower absenteeism, and 88% reporting easier recruitment.

Other studies have shown that a program of flexible scheduling likewise reduces absenteeism, lowers the turnover rate, eliminates tardiness, and improves morale and productivity.

A variety of programs for the working family are being pioneered by forward-looking employers. If your employer is not yet among them, the following descriptions of child-care arrangements, flexible scheduling, part-time jobs, and parental-leave policies may give you some ideas. And if some of the policies seem unsuited to your small office, perhaps your employer could team up with several other small firms to offer a benefit jointly.

Child-Care Arrangements

Some employers provide on-site child-care centers. Others make cash contributions, either to working parents or to neighborhood day-care centers, to ease the financial burden of child care. Polaroid Corporation, for example, issues vouchers that can be used to pay for any child-care arrangement of the parents' choosing. When

9 to 5 conducted a survey in which employees indicated a need for quality day care, the John Hancock Insurance Company donated $100,000 to local child-care centers and resources. Another program offered by a few employers is the "cafeteria plan," in which the employee receives a core of benefits and chooses additional benefits from among two or more alternatives, including provisions for child care, educational assistance, or extra health insurance.

Of particular assistance to working parents who are seeking child-care arrangements is an employer-run information and referral service, an up-to-date list of local child-care centers and family day-care homes. Some such services also screen day-care providers so that parents can approach them with confidence.

A working parent's greatest headache can occur when a child is sick or at home on vacation. A few companies have established day camps for school-age children on company-owned recreation property, administered by an organization such as the YWCA. A sick-child-care program is also helpful to working parents. Such a program run by Child Care Services/Health Care Services, Inc., in the Minneapolis–St. Paul area makes trained child-care workers available to employees on short notice.

Some employers run lunchtime parent seminars covering such topics as managing work and family responsibilities, finding good-quality child care, and identifying community resources for the working parent. (Employees can also start these groups themselves.)

Flexible Scheduling Provisions

Flex-time is a work schedule in which workers may choose arrival and departure times within certain limits. All employees work during a core period, and each employee arranges a daily schedule from the flexible periods to add up to the total required hours. For example, you might decide to work from 7:30 to 3:30 so that your husband can get the children off to school while you look after them when they come home. At some workplaces, the employee may vary the length of her workday as long as she works during the core period and puts in a set number of hours per week. The U.S. Department of Labor estimates that one worker in eight already uses alternative work schedules in one form or another.

Other nontraditional schedules can also be helpful. For example, in the Boston area Hewlett-Packard established a "working-parent shift" after a survey showed that many employees preferred to arrive home earlier in the afternoon to be with their school-age children. In the compressed work week, workers distribute their forty hours among three or four days rather than the traditional five. Such scheduling allows two parents to "cover" their children during the work week with a minimal need for outside child care. The disadvantage of this plan is that it can be hard to perform a stressful job for so many hours per day. In this and in flex-time arrangements, employees should be careful not to forfeit their rights to overtime pay.

Part-time jobs can also be helpful to working parents. They are now difficult to find, and the pay averages 20% less per hour than for full-time work. Part-timers seldom receive fringe benefits, paid vacations, health coverage, pension coverage, or unemployment compensation. Portable pensions and prorated benefits would make part-time work a far more attractive option for those who could afford the lower income.

In job-sharing arrangements, two employees split a

single job, each working half the hours. While the employer may incur extra unemployment- and medical-insurance costs, he can gain the top performance of two people, and they, of course, gain the time needed for child care.

PARENTAL-LEAVE POLICIES

There is a need, too, for a more flexible parental-leave system. Employers are legally required to treat pregnancy like any other temporary disability, and they may not discriminate against you on the basis of your condition. Some state laws guarantee a specified period of maternity leave during which your job must be held open and your seniority preserved. Beyond this, what is needed is a paid maternity leave lasting several weeks, including leave for adoptive parents. In many companies, it would be feasible to follow this with either an unpaid child-care leave period lasting several months or reduced work hours immediately after the maternity leave. Such a policy would benefit not only the parents but the employer as well, assuring the return of a qualified, trained employee and saving him the effort and expense of recruiting a permanent replacement.

Finally, there is a need for the extension of a parent's sick-leave provisions to include a child's illness. As long as they are unable to use sick days for the care of their sick children, many parents must either leave their sick children home alone, lie and say they themselves are sick, or use their vacation time.

"Spending the day with a sick child is certainly not a vacation," says Gail M. of Washington, D.C. "It is probably worse than being sick yourself. We should have the option to take sick leave when a family member is ill and our services as a mother and a health provider are needed."

Added to such sick-leave benefits could be extra personal leave time for participation in child-rearing activities such as doctor visits or teacher conferences.

Employers who provide benefits to aid the working family are few and far between. It is possible that as the advantages of such policies become more generally recognized, more companies will adopt them. Indeed, *Business Week* predicts that by 1990 child-care benefits will be as common as health benefits are today. But in spite of this optimistic view, much remains to be done. Working parents will have to exert pressure on their employers for the policies we need.

Circulating a questionnaire among working parents at your company is a good way to begin identifying which programs might be appropriate. Ask about the number and the ages of their children, the kind of child care they use, and the particular problems they encounter both at work and at home. (Keeping the questionnaire anonymous will make it possible for employees to admit their "illegal" use of sick days and the like without fear of reprisal.) Then list some possible programs the employer might inaugurate and ask respondents to indicate their degree of interest in each.

The compiled results of the questionnaire will give your employer a good idea about what programs to consider and will help avoid costly errors, such as setting up an on-site child-care center and finding that no one wants it. When you discuss your needs and options, refer your employer to a pamphlet published by the Department of Labor, *Employers and Child Care: Establishing Services Through the Workplace* (Women's Bureau, U.S. DOL, August 1982, Pamphlet 23).

The most effective way to ensure that your employer

offers the benefits you need is to have them guaranteed through a union contract. If you have a union, you may need to be active in it to get such policies placed high on the priority list during contract negotiations.

Through the Service Employees International Union, West Coast hospital workers formed a committee to investigate child-care alternatives and issued a report on the findings. Management at the large medical complex where they worked agreed to begin an information and referral service and to develop proposals for a voucher program, an on-site child-care center, and funding of neighborhood centers.

PUBLIC POLICIES

Not only our employers but also our elected officials need to hear from us about our needs for child care and other programs to ease the problems experienced by working parents. During World War II, the federal government joined with private industry to provide child care so that women could join the labor force. After the war, this program was discontinued on the assumption that women would leave the work force. Now that women are back in record numbers, the need for such a program has re-emerged.

In 1971 the Comprehensive Child Development Act was passed by Congress to provide planning and funding for child-care programs. Although the law was called "as important a breakthrough for the young as Medicare was for the old," it was vetoed by President Nixon. Currently the federal government provides limited subsidies for child-care facilities for low-income families, tax incentives for employers who provide child-care benefits, and child-care tax credits for working parents. Some states also subsidize child-care services.

In addition, the federal government and some state governments have instituted flexible schedules, job-sharing, and part-time work for public employees, and these have served as examples for the private sector.

But all these programs put together don't begin to address the enormous need for high-quality day-care arrangements or the need for corporate policies that aid the working family. Laws in many other countries are far better.

For example, in the United States maternity leave with full pay is a rarity, yet this situation would be considered backward in Brazil, where the United Nations reports that workers are entitled to twelve weeks of maternity leave with full pay. Kenya mandates eight weeks of paid leave. Most European countries offer more generous maternity leave than the United States. Many countries also require employers to provide half-hour nursing breaks for mothers of infants, and some grant extended periods of unpaid leave without loss of job rights.

FINDING CHILD CARE

Long before you go to work—either returning as a new mother or starting as a newcomer to the work force—you will need to research suitable child-care arrangements. The search may be difficult. In 1978 *Family Circle* magazine conducted a survey of mothers who were working full-time and had children under the age of thirteen. Of these, nearly a third had had to change child-care arrangements in the previous two years because the care was undependable or of poor quality. According to the same study, at least one-third of

school-age children of working mothers are home alone
after school, though 99% of their mothers were dissatis-
fied with this arrangement and would not continue it if
there were other options.

Sources for locating child-care situations are many.
You might want to start by talking with other working
parents about their arrangements. Exchanging information can help to allay worries and fears and give you
ideas on how to proceed. You can also check neighborhood bulletin boards and the want-ad column in your
local paper, or run an ad of your own if you don't find
what you want. Consult the Yellow Pages for day-care
centers and nursery schools. Community agencies,
churches, and the state office for children often have
lists of approved day-care arrangements.

For a preschool child, options you can choose from
include arranging your schedule so that your child's
father or another relative can look after him or her;
hiring a babysitter to care for your child—and possibly
others as well—either in her home or in yours; starting
a cooperative arrangement in which members work
part-time and rotate child care in their own homes; or
finding a day-care center or nursery school with long
hours.

Before you start looking, think about what you want.
Experts stress that the basis of good child care is a
warm and friendly relationship, both between child and
caregiver and between parent and caregiver. Try to
choose a program run by someone whose attitudes on
child care closely correspond to your own. Is it important to you that your child be cuddled and held a lot?
Are learning and structured stimulation high priorities?
How about contact with other children, or how convenient the arrangements are for your own schedule? Gov-
erning all these options, of course, is the ever-present
concern about what child care will cost.

Before settling on any arrangement, it is important to check references carefully and to conduct detailed interviews to discuss such matters as schedules, discipline, play, naps, feedings, and health and safety. Use the checklist on page 116 to evaluate situations you are considering. You probably won't find a solution that is ideal in every way, but comparing the "scores" of several options will help you make your choice.

Assume that the first two weeks or so of any plan you settle on will be a trial run. At the end of that time, assess whether your child is happy with the arrangement. If not, admit that it isn't working out and look for something else.

Once children begin to attend school, a variety of arrangements is possible. For example, a group of parents may hire one person to serve as companion for several children, supervising them in one home or in different homes on a rotating basis. Churches, community centers, and schools may run after-school programs.

By the time children are ten or eleven years old, many parents feel confident allowing them to stay home alone after school. If you have made this decision, make certain that there are activities to fill your child's time while you are away and that he or she is adequately trained in emergency procedures. Post a list of important numbers next to the phone, and make arrangements for having your child call you at work if necessary.

HOUSEHOLD POLICIES

Once you've taken care of your family responsibilities while you're away on the job, it's time to consider what

CHECKLIST FOR EVALUATING CHILD-CARE ARRANGEMENTS

HEALTH AND SAFETY

	YES	NO
Is the setting clean and attractive?	☐	☐
Is at least one adult present at all times?	☐	☐
Are household cleansers and drugs kept out of reach?	☐	☐
Are toys, furniture, and equipment sturdy and in good repair?	☐	☐

MATERIALS AND ACTIVITIES

Can children run and climb both indoors and outdoors?	☐	☐
Can children reach the play materials and choose from among several activities much of the time?	☐	☐
Are there arrangements for quiet play and a darkened room for naps?	☐	☐

CAREGIVERS

Are enough adults available so that children can receive individual attention?	☐	☐
Are the caregivers trained in child development?	☐	☐
Do the caregivers speak in terms children can understand and gain their cooperation through encouragement and praise?	☐	☐

CHILDREN

Do the children appear happy and busy?	☐	☐
Do they interact together in small groups?	☐	☐

Note: *A Parent's Guide to Day Care* is available free of charge from the U.S. Department of Health and Human Services, Washington, D.C., 20003 (Publication #80-30254, U.S. HHW, March 1980).

happens when you come home. The responsibilities you assume when you open your front door at supper time may surpass those you've been handling all day at the office. How do you take care of them all?

First, share the work load. Second, establish routines and stick to them. And third, lower your sights: don't expect everything to go smoothly all the time.

For those women who have run the household by themselves for years, surrendering such control may be difficult at first. Yet the family as a whole will benefit. If your children are old enough to assume responsibilities, they will enjoy a sense of maturity and become independent more quickly.

Whether you're coming to this reorganization of family tasks as a new mother or at a later stage, try to include as many family members as possible in the change. They are more likely to carry out tasks if they have had a say in making assignments. Once the assignments are made, hold firm. If you believe the new arrangement can work, it will.

Following routines will be easier if you narrow down your priorities. Many working mothers relax their standards of tidiness and cleanliness out of necessity; rarely does this cause problems.

Since the morning is the most frantic time of day, try to do as many things as you can the night before. In the evening, don't plan too much while your children are awake; spend some time playing with them or hearing about their day. Keep your meals simple.

You will probably want to spend some of your weekend time catching up on household chores—running errands, shopping, and cooking and freezing dinners for the days ahead—but keep in mind that it is important to allow some time for relaxation. Particularly if you are a single parent, it is essential that you set aside time for yourself and your own needs. You will be more efficient

both at home and at work if you allow yourself a rest
now and then.

As things now stand, many women in our society are
faced with an unfortunate and limited set of choices. We
can be a full-time housewife (if we can afford it) or a
full-time worker without children or a double-time "su-
permom." If the business world would recognize the
talents of women and the needs of parents, we would see
policies that took both children's and parents' needs
into account. We could be breadwinners without worry-
ing that our children were getting inadequate care, and
caring parents without having to give up our roles in the
work world. The old family stereotype could be laid to
rest and a more satisfying reality could take its place.
Working parents must make their voices heard toward
that end.

7.
Planning for Your Later Years

Like me, many of my friends and coworkers have years of service and experience. Without exception, our daughters earn more than we do.
—*Bank clerk in Providence, Rhode Island*

People say that life begins at forty, but for working women, this saying is far from the truth. Older women who have put in years of dedicated service to the companies they work for get passed up for promotions and raises, train younger men to do more highly paid jobs, and retire with a tiny pension or no pension at all to live out their remaining years in poverty.
—*62-year-old woman worker in St. Louis*

LUCILLE H., a Baltimore widow in her fifties, decided to perform an experiment to educate herself and her fellow 9 to 5 members about the realities of retirement income. She came up with a plan to try living on her projected retirement income for two weeks. Lucille knew she could economize. She planned to shop carefully and keep her grocery bill very low. She sat down to compute her retirement income. After six years of employment in the federal government, she figured she would receive a pension of $57.29 per month. To this she added her widow's Social Security benefits of $148.50, for a total of $206.09. Lucille was shocked. Her rent bill alone would exceed her entire monthly income. She realized that living on her retirement income would be far more difficult than she had imagined.

Lucille's experiment bears out the facts about older women, the fastest-growing poverty group in America today. According to the Department of Labor, nearly one out of every five older women is poor. Those who expect their husbands to support them upon retirement are often caught short: most women outlive their husbands, and many widows who expect to collect their husbands' pension benefits cannot do so. Nearly one-third of all women over 55 depend on their own income alone.

Two key factors make it difficult for women to attain a level of security when they retire. First, the low pay and lack of advancement opportunities that afflict us throughout our careers result in meager Social Security and pension benefits and in an inability to put savings aside. And second, whatever the size of our earnings, both Social Security and the pension system are profoundly unsuited to women's career patterns.

Far from being rewarded for years of experience, many women find that their job problems only get worse after the age of 40. Older women are stereotyped as cranky, bossy, and sickly. At the very age when many executive men are entering the prime of their careers, we're considered over the hill.

Sociological studies actually disprove the notion that young women make better employees than older women. For example, according to the American Council of Life Insurance, workers age 45 and older used 3.1 sick days in 1979, less time than their younger colleagues, who used 3.7 days. The turnover rate for women in their early fifties is only one-sixth the rate for women in their twenties.

Yet older women encounter barriers in looking for a job, experience discrimination in pay and other aspects of employment, and meet with pressure to retire earlier than they want to.

Job hunting can be a nightmare for women over 40. "No one will hire you when you are fifty-three, even with twelve good years of work ahead of you," said one top-notch executive secretary who had been looking for a job for over a year.

In one Midwestern city, a male supporter of 9 to 5, posing as an employer, called a dozen employment agencies. "We have a young sales staff on the move," he said. "We want a woman with the right image who will fit in—someone attractive and under twenty-five." Even though it is illegal to fill an order that discriminates against older workers, nine of the twelve agencies accepted the request.

"You can specify any age," one agency representative responded, "but it's so hard to tell. These ladies can do miracles with cosmetics and a good hairdo."

"Do you want a blonde or brunette?" another asked bluntly.

As for pay, in blue-collar fields the wage differential between an employee with ten years of seniority and one with twenty-five years often amounts to thousands of dollars. But the salary structure of clerical work does not reward experience. According to the Department of Labor, older women as a group earn only $71 more per year than younger women. One government study even showed that the economic status of many women re-entering the work force after child-rearing is *lower* than it was in their youth.

"I'm making only ten cents an hour more than kids

just coming in," said a Cincinnati insurance worker. "When I get my next annual raise, I'll be at the top of the salary level for my job category with nowhere to go. Then what? Do I stop advancing at forty-three?"

Older women are often denied access to training and promotion opportunities because of their age. "They don't want to 'waste' training on a fifty-year-old," one secretary explained.

In a 9 to 5 survey of women with at least five years in the work force, one-third said they had lost out on a promotion in favor of a younger person with less experience. Employers sometimes cite "lack of degree" as a reason for denying advancement. "They just rewrote the job description for the job I've done for years and added 'college degree required' to the description," said an advertising-agency employee. "I couldn't get my own job back if I applied for it today!"

Older women also encounter pressure to retire, ranging from subtle hints to denial of promotions or raises to outright firing. Why? If an employer is undergoing a reduction in his work force, he'll save money by terminating older employees, who may be closer to being eligible to collect pension benefits.

A Baton Rouge woman had worked for one company for twenty-eight years, ten of them as secretary to the president. She and the president took their yearly vacations at the same time. When she returned a few weeks before her boss, she was told he had left a message concerning her.

"I'm sorry to have to tell you this," a coworker said to her, "but the boss doesn't want you out front anymore because you've put on a few pounds. You're being transferred to acquisitions."

"But I'm an executive secretary!" the woman protested. "I don't know anything about acquisitions."

She refused to take the position in which she had no

expertise and was fired—two years before she would have received full pension benefits.

A highly respected secretary with years of experience may find her job security evaporating when her boss moves on or retires. A 54-year-old San Antonio woman tells this story:

> I liked my job and I worked hard, staying late to get things done. Everyone said how competent I was. My trouble began when I got a new boss, who began to pick at little things, saying I talked too much on the phone, or I shouldn't read the newspaper, or I was disorganized.
>
> Finally I received a scathing memo from him which made it clear I'd have to quit. I was stunned. I had so much experience and knew so many things about that place. I was distraught, furious, miserable. If I hadn't gotten another job right away, I would have felt even worse.
>
> It could have been my age, or the benefits I was getting because of my experience, or it could be he wanted a younger woman to chase around the desk. It could have been all of those things.

Such unfair treatment of older women is a problem in its own right. But discriminatory employment practices also keep earnings and savings so low that it is difficult for women to amass an adequate retirement income. The retirement system itself also poses many problems for women.

When Social Security was established in the 1930s, experts talked about the "three-legged stool" approach to retirement income, with private pension and personal savings supplying the other two legs. But, in fact, Social Security benefits, which are tiny, constitute the sole income of most single women over 65, according to the Social Security Administration.

To become eligible to collect retirement benefits, you must work for approximately forty quarters, or ten years, in employment covered by Social Security, which includes most jobs. These do not have to be consecutive years or quarters, and if you were born before 1929 you'll need fewer years. When you retire, you receive benefits based on your earnings over a period of years. Benefits increase automatically as the cost of living rises. You will receive full benefits if you retire at age 65. If you retire as early as age 62, your payments will be reduced by about 20%; if you retire after age 65, you will receive higher benefits.

The Social Security system harbors many problems for women. Widows receive no dependents' benefits until age 60, unless they are severely disabled or have children who are still minors. Divorced women must have been married to the retired worker for ten years to receive benefits.

Further, a woman can collect on either her own earnings record or on the record of her husband, whichever will yield more money. Since women generally earn significantly less than men over the course of their work lives, the spouse's benefit—about 50% of the husband's benefit—is usually higher than the amount she is entitled to under her own earnings credit. Although she has paid into the system for years, she may receive no more than she would have if she had never worked outside the home at all.

Finally, many retired women and men find Social Security payments inadequate to live on. But the Social Security law acts as a disincentive for them to supplement their income. If you earn more than the several-thousand-dollar limit in a given year, you lose benefits.

If Social Security fails to meet the needs of women retirees, the pension system is far worse. Nearly 70% of the women workers in private industry are not covered by pension plans at all, and many of those who are covered never collect a penny.

Many plans require you to work for your employer for ten years before you "vest," or become eligible for benefits upon retirement. That means that if you quit your job after nine years, you may forfeit your pension. Vesting requirements are a severe handicap for women in low-paying, high-turnover jobs. They are particularly hard on women with child-rearing responsibilities; those who leave the work force to raise children commonly forfeit their accumulated benefits.

The small minority of women who do collect pensions receive an average of only $80 per month. Pension benefits are based on earnings; women's lower pay is reflected in lower pension benefits. And in some cases—though this has been challenged in court—women's monthly payments are smaller than men's, on the assumption that women will live longer.

Few pension plans are indexed to inflation. If you begin collecting $157 a month when you retire, you'll continue collecting $157 twenty years later, even if by then such a sum will buy you only a can of beans and a bus ride downtown. If there is a steep rise in the inflation, a pension could become nearly valueless after a period of fifteen years.

When your husband retires, he may decide to collect a larger pension benefit while he is alive rather than collect a reduced sum during his lifetime and provide a widow's benefit for you after his death. He does not have to inform you of his decision. And unless you have been married to your husband for a full year before he starts collecting his pension and a full year before he dies, you are not entitled to any widow's benefits, even if he wanted you to have them. Further, as a divorced wife, whether you may share his pension while he is alive depends entirely upon the terms of your divorce decree.

A major private-pension-reform law that was passed in 1974—the Employee Retirement Income Security Act—corrected some past inequities. But many women working today suffer from practices predating the law. For example, before the law took effect it was legal to exclude employees from coverage if they were hired after age 45. Many such workers will not be eligible for benefits when they retire, in spite of the new law.

Too many women fail to think about their retirement until it is almost upon them. Given the many factors operating against us, both in the work world and in the retirement system, such delay can be a grave mistake. Begin today to protect yourself from the prospect of retiring into poverty.

First, make retirement planning a part of your career decisions throughout your lifetime. No matter what your age, ask a potential employer about the pension plan when you are considering taking a job. Likewise, as you plan to leave a job, consider the effect this will have on your pension. You may find that postponing your departure by a few months or a year could make an enormous difference in your retirement security.

Ask these questions of your employer or prospective employer:

- Am I/would I be covered by a pension plan?
- How long must I work in order to be eligible for pension benefits when I retire?
- At what age can I receive full retirement benefits? Reduced benefits?
- How large will my monthly check be after ___ years of work?
- Is this plan insured by the federal government?
- What is the normal retirement age under this pension plan? The early retirement age?

- If I receive pension benefits, how large will my monthly check be?

Second, learn to analyze and build your retirement income. You may want to seek retirement counseling on such topics as accurately predicting the size of your retirement income and budget, maximizing your savings, deciding when to retire, and working part-time after retirement. Ask your personnel manager if he or she will provide for such counseling for you and your coworkers.

Figure out how much income you will need in order to retire in comfort. Think ahead and envision your ideal retirement life-style. Remember that Social Security and pension benefits will replace only part of your pre-retirement income and that inflation may take a heavy toll on your savings.

You can use the "rule of 72"—an investment formula—to determine how much money you are likely to need in the future. Estimate the annual inflation rate and divide that number into 72 to tell how long it will be before your financial needs will double. For example, a woman of 48 who has an annual income of $12,500 estimates her income needs at age 65, when she plans to retire. She predicts that the inflation rate will average 8% per year. Dividing 8 into 72, she learns that it will be 9 years before she will need twice as much as she earns now—that is, $25,000 a year. And 18 years from now, at retirement age, she will need approximately $50,000 a year if she is to maintain the same standard of living.

Become aware of the benefits you are accruing. Your local Social Security office can tell you how much you have earned at any point, and your employer must furnish you with an annual statement of your accrued pension benefits. And ask your spouse these questions:

- Am I covered by your pension plan?
- Will I be covered if you die before you retire, or before you reach age 55?
- Should we opt for survivor's benefits, even though this will mean a lower pension payment while we are both alive?

Finally, in building your retirement income, educate yourself about investing your savings wisely. Many of us with little to invest tend to put our money into "safe" vehicles. But safe is not so safe if the money is guaranteed to lose purchasing power. Savings accounts, savings bonds, some annuity policies, and life insurance savings policies provide a fixed rate of return which is often lower than the rate of inflation.

There are many other options for the small saver. Factors to consider in choosing an investment option are the amount of interest your investment will earn, the minimum deposit required, the length of time your money will be tied up (if at all), penalties for early withdrawal, and the degree of risk involved. A popular handbook such as Mary Elizabeth Schlayer's *How to Be a Financially Secure Woman* can help you choose the options you feel comfortable with.

Women with small savings should investigate credit union savings accounts, 90-day special-notice accounts, certificates of deposit available through banks, mutual funds, money-market certificates, and money-market cash-reserve accounts.

There is a third step women need to take if we are to achieve job satisfaction in our later working years and maximize our chances of having a secure retirement. We need to take action to stop the dual discrimination based on age and sex that plagues women workers over 40, and we must work toward correcting the problems in our retirement system.

Older workers have been successful in pushing their employers to establish better policies. For example, older workers in one Southern city held an informal public hearing on the problems they faced and garnered considerable press coverage for their testimony about the ways pension-vesting requirements penalize women. After the hearing, the employees at a major bank were able to persuade management to lower the vesting requirement from ten to five years and to increase the size of the benefits. In a Midwestern city, women met with the personnel director of a major department store and won similar improvements as well as a retirement counseling program.

When such informal pressure is not effective, older workers have found the Age Discrimination in Employment Act to be a useful tool. This federal law, like many state laws, prohibits discrimination in hiring, firing, training, promotion, and pay against persons between ages 40 and 70. When a New York insurance company terminated 550 employees in 1978 and 1979, laid-off workers over 40 joined together to charge that the firings were being used to weed out qualified older employees. The case, believed to be the largest such action yet filed in the United States, is still pending.

In another instance, a bank laid off thirty-five employees, all of whom were over 40. About a month later, the bank advertised openings for their positions and hired replacements, all of whom were under 40. An age-discrimination charge filed on behalf of twenty-five of the employees resulted in a settlement of $250,000 in back pay.

Unionizing is another way to protect yourself against age discrimination. In fact, protection of long-term employees has been one of the major demands of unions throughout the history of the labor movement.

At a Midwestern community college, an employee in

her fifties sat idly in a corner of the campus library for weeks while the administration figured out what to do with her during a reorganization. On another occasion, twenty-five employees, some of them with fifteen years' experience, were suddenly ordered with no explanation to reapply for their own positions. Some failed to get the jobs they had been doing for years and ended up in other departments with lower salaries. In addition to suffering as a result of these arbitrary actions, older women were particularly affected when their supervisors played favorites. On one occasion, two older women with five and ten years' seniority had their hours cut back to part-time while the hours of a part-timer in the same department were increased.

Issues like these led the clerical staff at the college to unionize with 9 to 5's sister union, District 925 of the Service Employees International Union, and long-term employees were among the strongest supporters of the drive. "The important issue for most of us was job security," Barbara S. said. "Finally we have a voice. Once we have our union contract, no one will be able to walk in and say, 'We don't want you here anymore.' The closer I get to retirement, the more I feel a need for that kind of protection."

Whether through informal pressure or persuasion, a discrimination charge, or a union, women workers can encourage employers to improve their treatment of older women through these model personnel policies. Employers should:

- take measures to eliminate age discrimination in hiring, promotion, training, and firing;
- create career ladders enabling older women to move up;
- institute job posting;

- provide promotions and training for older women at a rate at least commensurate with their participation in the company work force;
- remove artificial educational requirements whenever on-the-job experience is a satisfactory indication of job qualification;
- restructure clerical wage scales to reward experience and eliminate low salary ceilings;
- institute regular merit and cost-of-living increases;
- provide retirement counseling;
- institute pension coverage with quick vesting for all employees.

In addition to pressing employers, we must make our elected representatives aware that the retirement system needs an overhaul. There are a number of proposals before Congress that aim to eliminate the inequities of the Social Security system and ensure that benefits are more adequate. Pension law reforms have also been proposed, requiring provisions to reflect the actual work patterns of the majority of the work force, such as immediate vesting. Others propose that pension benefits should be preserved during breaks in service such as child-rearing leaves, that an employee's spouse should have to consent to the waiving of survivor's benefits, and that pension coverage should be prorated for part-time workers.

None of us can afford to ignore the problems of older women in the work force and the injustices that riddle our retirement-income system. But if we begin now to shape our careers wisely and take action to combat the problems, perhaps each of us can achieve the secure retirement that now may be only a dream.

8.
The Office Worker's Bill of Rights

I never thought about my job rights until I was fired for no good reason. I was furious and ready to file a lawsuit against my boss. I was even more furious when I found that the law didn't protect me one bit.
—*New Orleans office manager*

Years ago I worked at a firm where we all stayed late into the evening week after week and never got paid extra for it. We even had to bring our own sandwiches for dinner. To this day I regret that none of us knew about the right to overtime pay. I'm still thinking about how I could have spent that money.
—*Houston secretary*

OFFICE workers do have rights—some, anyway—including the right to improve our working conditions. Knowing these rights and how to use them increases the likelihood that we will be treated fairly at work.

Historically, the United States has upheld a belief in fairness and equality, though this ethic is often violated. The unwritten law of the workplace is that everyone deserves a fair shake. The legal rights we have today grew out of our forebears' conviction that they were being treated unjustly and the fight they waged to win redress. Our right to organize came from the labor movement of the 1930s. Antidiscrimination laws grew out of the civil rights movement of the 1950s and 1960s. Health and safety laws sprang from the efforts of organized industrial workers in the 1970s.

So if you think something is unfair, whether it's legal or illegal, hang on to your outrage. It *is* wrong for your boss to fire you without warning, even if it's not yet illegal.

Once a law is on the books, frequent use makes it effective. For example, since the passage of the Civil Rights Act in 1964, tens of thousands of companies have been charged with bias against women and minorities, and back-pay settlements and policy changes have ensued. Some of the cases have involved huge settlements and considerable publicity, and as a result, even employers who have not been sued have re-examined their employment policies and taken steps to eliminate bias.

As employers change their policies to conform to equal employment guidelines, many are surprised to discover that their businesses operate more efficiently. According to a report (*Improving Job Opportunities for Women* by Ruth Gilbert Shaeffer and Helen Axel) issued by The Conference Board, a nonprofit business study group, "Many major employers now say that . . . equal employment opportunity makes good business sense; that this country can no longer afford to waste such a valuable natural resource as the vast pool of human potential our various minorities and females represent. Together these . . . groups account for just about half the civilian work force."

Of course, while many employers have changed, many others have not. Some have just become more

DO YOU KNOW YOUR RIGHTS?

Under the law, can your employer:

		YES	NO
1.	Provide better health coverage for the professional employees who are mainly men than for the clericals who are women?	☐	☐
2.	Promise you two weeks' vacation when you were hired but actually give you only one?	☐	☐
3.	Have you working for one man for the past three years, then suddenly give you the work of two more?	☐	☐
4.	Threaten to fire you for filing a sex discrimination claim against the company?	☐	☐
5.	Require you to do personal errands for your boss?	☐	☐
6.	Lay off employees for economic reasons arbitrarily, with no attention to seniority or competence?	☐	☐
7.	Make it almost impossible for an employee who is dissatisfied with her job to get a transfer?	☐	☐
8.	Give a bigger salary (and a different title) to the man next to you, who has similar qualifications and does the same work?	☐	☐
9.	Threaten to fire you for talking to other employees about unionizing?	☐	☐
10.	Refuse to pay time and a half for overtime because the profit-sharing plan makes up for it?	☐	☐
11.	Neglect to set up any procedure for the secretaries to bring their grievances to management?	☐	☐
12.	Require women to leave in the sixth month of pregnancy?	☐	☐

Answers:

1) yes   2) yes   3) yes   4) no   5) yes   6) yes   7) yes
8) no   9) no   10) no   11) yes   12) no

How well did you do? How well did your employer do?

wily in using discriminatory practices that are designed to save money, exclude women or minorities, or preserve the "old boys'" tradition of dealing only with their own kind.

To be sure, unequal treatment of women workers is still widespread. But public opinion is against discrimination, and increasingly we office workers are standing up for our rights. Whether it is through lawsuits, memos, unionizing, meetings, or whatever other activities you choose, make it your business to be treated fairly.

One of the first items on 9 to 5's agenda when we began organizing ten years ago was the development of a Bill of Rights for Women Office Workers. Some elements of these rights are currently guaranteed by law; others may be soon. And some may always be a matter of negotiation between employer and employee. Rate your employer. If he falls short, you are within your rights to do something about it.

Often, just knowing your rights will enable you to act with confidence in insisting upon fair treatment. In other situations, reminding your boss of the laws' provisions can put a stop to illegal treatment. The threat of legal action, particularly when combined with other forms of organized pressure, can be effective in guaranteeing your rights. And as a last resort, be aware of the procedures for formal legal action.

If you feel that your rights are being infringed upon at work, first try to remedy the situation without resorting to legal action. Discuss your problem with your boss. Give him an opportunity to develop a reasonable solution to your complaint. If he won't, tell him that you would like to take the matter up with his superior, and do so. Remember that the mere possibility of legal action may produce speedy improvements.

If you are considering legal action, keep records re-

THE 9 TO 5 BILL OF RIGHTS

The right to respect as women and as workers.

The right to fair and adequate compensation, based on performance and length of service; regular salary reviews; and cost-of-living increases.

The right to written, accurate job descriptions specifying all job duties, and the right to choose whether to do the personal work of employers.

The right to fair and equal access to promotion opportunities, including a job-posting program announcing all openings and training programs that give each employee an opportunity for job growth.

The right to a say over office policies, and the right to participate in organizing to improve our status.

The right to an effective, systematic grievance procedure.

The right to fair treatment in every aspect of employment without regard to sex, age, race, or sexual preference.

garding your complaint, and maintain a good work record. While it may be difficult to keep up your performance standards when you are feeling mistreated, any erosion of your work will give your employer the perfect alibi for his illegal actions. Discuss the situation with your coworkers. If they have similar complaints, your case may be stronger. Before you take any action, seek support and advice from your union, a women's or civil rights organization like 9 to 5, or a legal aid clinic.

EQUAL EMPLOYMENT OPPORTUNITY

Several laws guarantee equal treatment on the job.

1. *Title VII of the Civil Rights Act of 1964* prohibits discrimination in employment based on sex, race, color,

religion, and national origin. The act covers hiring, firing, wages, fringe benefits, assigning, classifying, training, and promoting employees, and all other terms, conditions, and privileges of employment. It covers most employers of fifteen or more employees, employment agencies, and unions with fifteen or more members.

Title VII also prohibits sexual harassment. If you are unable to stop harassment by taking action within your company, you can file charges. (You may also be able to bring a harasser who assaults you to court.)

2. *The Equal Pay Act of 1963* prohibits unequal pay and benefits for men and women who work in the same establishment and whose jobs require equal skill, effort, and responsibility. (Pay differentials may be deemed fair if they are based on seniority, merit, or quantity or quality of production.) A number of court cases have established that jobs need be only substantially equal, not identical, in order to be covered by the act.

3. *The Pregnancy Discrimination Act of 1978* gives pregnant women the same legal rights as other employees. The law says that employers cannot refuse to hire or promote a pregnant woman who is capable of performing the job adequately, demote or fire a woman because of pregnancy, or force a woman to take a leave of absence if she can still work. A few states, such as Massachusetts, require employers to go further and grant a minimum amount of maternity leave—for example, eight weeks.

Once you are no longer able to work because of pregnancy or childbirth, you are entitled to disability benefits or sick leave on the same basis as employees who are unable to work because of other temporary disabilities. For example, when Jim S. breaks his leg on a skiing vacation, his employer grants him disability leave and part of his salary while he is recovering. Jim also retains his seniority while he is away. In the same way, while Mary J. is disabled by pregnancy and childbirth, she should receive the same disability leave and partial pay, and retain her seniority. On the other hand, an employer who does not provide any benefits for workers disabled by broken bones doesn't have to do so for pregnant workers either, unless state law requires it. Check with your state government to see whether you might be eligible for state disability pay while you are on maternity leave.

4. *The Age Discrimination in Employment Act* prohibits discrimination on the basis of age against any person between the ages of 40 and 70, in hiring, firing, compensation, or other conditions of employment. The law applies to all public employers, private employers of twenty or more employees, employment agencies, and unions with more than twenty-five members.

5. *The Rehabilitation Act of 1973* provides that no qualified person shall be discriminated against on the basis of a mental or physical disability. The act covers hiring, promotion, training, benefits, and other conditions of employment. It prohibits employers from weeding out applicants by asking them to list their disabilities on job application forms. The enforcement mechanism for this law is complex. For further information, call the Disability Rights Education and Defense Fund in Berkeley, California. The toll-free number is 800-227-2472.

These laws are enforced primarily by the Equal Employment Opportunity Commission (EEOC). Many states also have fair-employment laws that forbid discrimination. These vary greatly; in some cases, the agencies that administer these laws provide quicker action than do the federal agencies. Check with the EEOC in your area or with the state attorney general.

If you take your case to the EEOC, you must file within 180 days of the discriminatory incident. State agencies may have different filing periods. Most agencies that combat discrimination require that you appear in person to file your charge. You may have to take a day off from work, since some agencies do not make appointments. Hiring a lawyer may not be a prerequisite for filing; the agencies are designed to be used without one. But keep in mind that your employer may very well retain a lawyer who is skilled in presenting the management side of employment cases. Your employer will be notified that you have filed a charge within ten working days. If he retaliates against you— by firing you, harassing you, demoting you, or the like— the enforcement agency can intervene and even seek a court order to stop the retaliation. Next, an EEOC investigator will bring you and your employer together at a fact-finding conference to ask questions and attempt to settle the matter. If this isn't successful, the agency may investigate further, calling or visiting your employer to review company documents. If it seems to the investigator that your charge has merit, the agency will try again to settle the matter with your employer. If the agency isn't successful, you have the right to file a suit on your own in court, with the help of an attorney.

How can you tell whether you are being discriminated against? Your employer probably won't come right out and tell you that you aren't qualified for a promotion because you're a woman. (If he does, he's definitely breaking the law.)

Discrimination may take a passive form. Your boss may keep forgetting about your desire to be trained in a new skill because he can't get it through his head that a woman would be interested in such a thing. If his bias is affecting your employment, your rights are being violated. Or discrimination may take a more aggressive form. Your boss may deliberately turn down your requests for training again and again, insisting that you are not qualified. Again, if what determines his actions is your sex, race, age, or disability, you're being discriminated against. If he'll accept tardiness in men but not in women, then he's acting illegally. If he's invariably critical of blacks but lets whites off easy, he's discriminating. If he tries to pressure employees to retire when they turn 55, he's acting illegally.

The first question you must ask yourself is why your employer is treating you badly. If he is a miserable person who is mean and nasty to men, women, young people, old people, whites, blacks, Asians, Hispanics, Catholics, Jews, Buddhists, Protestants, activists, and nonactivists alike, he's not guilty. If he won't promote people with glasses, he's not guilty. If he just dislikes you for no particular reason and does everything he can to keep you down, he's not guilty. To be acting illegally, he must treat you differently specifically because of your sex, race, disability, or age.

You may be experiencing illegal discrimination on the basis of sex, for example, if you find yourself in any of these circumstances:

- You are denied a job or promotion in favor of a man with less tenure and experience, particularly if you were the "natural" person for the job.
- You have trained men who now supervise you.
- In your company or department, jobs held mostly by men provide greater promotion potential than jobs held mostly by women.
- Most of the employees in your company or department are women, but most of the administrative jobs are held by men.

OUTLINE FOR A DISCRIMINATION CHARGE

This is not an official form; it is intended to help you determine whether you have experienced discrimination. If you file charges, this form will help you answer the questions of the agency representative who screens your application.

1. When did the incident occur? _____

2. Who was involved? (Give names and titles.) _____
   _____

3. What are the major points of your complaint?
   1. _____
   2. _____
   3. _____
   4. _____
   5. _____

4. Briefly describe what happened. _____
   _____
   _____
   _____
   _____

5. What kind of evaluations have you received? _____

6. Did other people witness this incident? _____ (Give names and titles.) _____
   _____

7. Was this incident the result of your age, sex, race, color, religion, national origin, handicap? _____
   _____

8. What makes you think so? _____

9. What explanation will your company give for the incident?
   _____

- You are not eligible for health and life insurance benefits that the wives of male employees receive.

You must be able to prove that you were not hired, not promoted, not trained, and so on primarily because you are a woman and that the person who *was* hired, trained, or promoted was a man. Your employer will seek to show that there was a legitimate and nondiscriminatory reason for his action—for example, an absenteeism problem. You can also claim that a general *policy* that affects you—such as a particular qualification for advancement that penalizes women—has a discriminatory impact on women or minorities in general at the company. The employer will counter by trying to show that the policy is necessary for sound business reasons.

Women often experience "dual discrimination," based on sex as well as age. For example, your employer may value older men and younger women but discriminate against older women. Older minority women can experience triple discrimination.

Jane G., a copy editor, was denied a raise on the basis that her personality was too aggressive. She maintained that this was a discriminatory excuse that would never have been used against a man. Within weeks after she filed a charge of discrimination, her company approached her with a raise and $1,800 in retroactive payments.

Edna C. had worked for a bank in her small town for twenty years and had been head cashier for some time. You can imagine her surprise when she discovered that a young man who had been with the bank for only a few years was earning $3,000 more than her $9,000-a-year salary. When she got over the shock, she filed charges with the state antidiscrimination agency. Within a year she had won over $50,000 in back pay for herself and six coworkers.

AFFIRMATIVE ACTION

Executive Order 11246 requires companies that have business contracts with the federal government to take positive action to correct the effects of past discriminatory employment practices. (A wide range of employers is covered. Publishers, for example, sell books to army-base schools. Banks serve as repositories for federal funds. Many companies are subcontractors—they do business with firms that hold contracts with the government.) Many such employers are required to write an Affirmative Action Plan and make it accessible to employees. Generally, you'll be able to read the Affirmative Action Plan in the personnel office. The plan will identify problem areas where women and minority group members are not sufficiently represented and will set goals and timetables for correcting these problems.

Executive Order 11246 is enforced by the Office of Federal Contract Compliance Programs (OFCCP) of the U.S. Department of Labor. OFCCP may conduct an on-site review of an employer, interview both management and employees about how the Affirmative Action Plan is working, and require the company to improve its efforts.

THE RIGHT TO ORGANIZE

The National Labor Relations Act (NLRA), passed in 1935, is designed to protect workers who take joint action to improve working conditions. Nonsupervisory, nonmanagerial employees in most private industry workplaces are covered by the act.

The NLRA defines the rights of employees to organize, including:

- Taking action as a group to improve conditions at the workplace, or attempting to take such actions. (Even if none of your coworkers will listen to you, you may be protected in your right to attempt to initiate group action.)
- Discussing a union or other such group whose aim is to improve working conditions; forming a union or other such group.
- Handing out leaflets or posting signs on a bulletin board in nonwork areas such as the cafeteria or the bathroom, on nonwork time such as before and after work, or during breaks and lunch hour.

The act is enforced by the National Labor Relations Board (NLRB), where you can ask for information about your right to organize, or file a charge. You must file within six months of the violation.

HEALTH

The Occupational Safety and Health Act (OSHA) of 1970 is designed to guarantee a safe and healthful place of employment to working women and men in the private sector. Federal government employees are similarly protected under Executive Order 11807, and many public employees on the state and local levels have other protection. Most OSHA standards are geared toward factories rather than offices. There are currently no federal standards for ventilation, heat, temperature, or lighting for nonindustrial settings, and few investigations of office health hazards are conducted.

The National Institute for Occupational Safety and Health (NIOSH) can perform a health hazard evaluation of your office. An investigator will test the workplace for causes of health complaints and make recommendations to alleviate the problems.

If you decide to file a complaint with either agency you may do so through your union, if you have one, or as an individual or a group of individuals. You may request anonymity. Make your complaint in writing and support it with as much information as possible.

WORKERS' COMPENSATION

Every state provides a system of weekly benefits for employees who have been disabled by a job injury. To collect, you must show that you are disabled and that your work or an incident at work caused your disability. (You don't have to show that it was the company's fault. For example, if you sustain an injury falling off a stepladder, you can collect benefits whether or not the ladder was flimsy.) It may be difficult to collect benefits for a job-related *disease*, as opposed to an *injury*, because many states require you to file a claim shortly after exposure to the hazard, even though some diseases take years to develop. In addition, some of the diseases common to office workers are only beginning to be recognized as job-related. Office workers are increasingly filing claims for stress-related diseases as society begins to recognize these as legitimate occupational hazards.

BREAKS

Under most state laws, employees are entitled to a thirty-minute break when they work more than six hours in one day.

MINIMUM WAGES AND OVERTIME PAY

The Fair Labor Standards Act covers the great majority of workers. Minimum hourly rates are raised periodically; check with the Wage and Hour Division of the U.S. Department of Labor for the latest figures.

Most workers are entitled to $1\frac{1}{2}$ times their regular rate of pay for hours in excess of 40 a week. (If you are paid by the month, hourly pay is calculated by dividing the monthly salary by the number of hours you normally work. And if you normally work 35 hours a week, or $37\frac{1}{2}$, you should be paid at straight salary up to 40 hours and $1\frac{1}{2}$ times your salary over 40.) Instead of overtime, your employer may give you compensatory time off during the pay period in which you work the overtime.

Most women workers qualify for overtime pay, though some executives, administrators, professionals, and outside sales employees are exempt. A few types of companies (such as railroads and airlines) are exempt as well, and some companies (such as hospitals) may compute overtime pay on a different basis.

UNEMPLOYMENT BENEFITS

Unemployment benefits are paid weekly for a limited time to eligible workers in order to tide them over between jobs when they are involuntarily unemployed. Each state administers its own program. Federal workers are covered by a special federal program.

You are eligible if:

- you have worked long enough in "covered" employment—which includes almost all jobs—to meet your state's requirements;
- you are not at fault in causing your unemployment; and
- you are able to work and can demonstrate that you have been actively seeking employment. Pregnant workers and new mothers are eligible if they meet these criteria.

To apply for benefits, go to the nearest unemployment insurance office. If you are found to be eligible, you'll receive a percentage—often 50%—of your average former wages. Many states limit coverage to a maximum of twenty-six weeks, but there may be extended benefits in times of high unemployment.

You may be determined ineligible for the following reasons:

- your employer lays you off or fires you for "just cause," such as a willful failure to perform your job adequately, a violation of a rule of employment, and so on;
- you quit solely due to pregnancy;
- you quit without "just cause."

"You can't fire me, I quit!" is the worst thing you can say if you hope to collect unemployment. However, you still may have a chance if you can show that circumstances forced you to leave your job.

If you are denied benefits, you may appeal within fourteen days. And if this appeal is denied, you may appeal again to a review board, where you can be represented by an attorney if you so choose.

Your employer may contest your right to receive benefits, since his payments into the unemployment fund may increase if your claim is granted.

SOCIAL SECURITY

Most workers are covered by Social Security upon retirement. The exact amount of your monthly benefits is determined when you apply for them upon retirement. Instead of drawing benefits in your own name, you may draw them as a dependent of your spouse; in such a case, you are entitled to payments totaling 50% of his monthly benefits. The Social Security office will let you know which arrangement would result in higher benefits.

If you are widowed or divorced, you may be eligible to

collect benefits, subject to special rules concerning the length of the marriage, remarriage, your age, and whether you are disabled. Your children will also be eligible in certain cases.

Your Social Security benefits are administered by the Social Security Administration. Call or write your local Social Security office to correct problems in the size of your benefits, to appeal the size of your benefits, or at any time before your retirement to check the size of your earnings to date or to check whether your employer has paid into your fund.

PENSIONS

The Employee Retirement Income Security Act (ERISA) of 1974 is a complex law designed to protect the interests of workers who participate in private pension plans.

ERISA sets standards for vesting of pension benefits. Under most plans, you must put in ten years of service at one company before the benefits are truly "yours" to collect upon retirement. In addition, the law requires your employer to provide you with a summary of the pension plan written in plain English. You are entitled to an annual statement of the total benefits you have accrued and the date on which you will become vested. In some cases, you'll receive this information automatically; in others, you'll have to make a written request.

For more information on pension rights, get in touch with the Labor Management Services Administration of the U.S. Department of Labor, or with the Pension Rights Center, 1346 Connecticut Avenue, N.W., Washington, D.C., 20036.

The risks of taking legal action are several. The process is slow and cumbersome, and many of the enforcement agencies have a poor record. You won't necessarily be able to file a charge, sit back, and let the wheels of justice turn. If you hire a lawyer, you may or may not make back your expenses when the case is settled. And because taking legal action is a strong, confrontational move, your employer may fight back with all he's got.

One woman had this to say after years of pursuing a case that has yet to be resolved: "Ten pounds, seven ounces and nine years later in briefs, papers, appeals, delays—nine years of frustration, tears, downright anger—I am still discriminated against and seemingly with no recourse except deep seething anger at the injustices still rampant against women."

On the other hand, legal action may be the only way you can win the redress you want. It can be particularly effective when used in combination with organizing. And if you do win, you'll feel great. Kay H. reports: "I've worked as a secretary for twenty years and just recently was awarded a large settlement by the Workers' Compensation Appeals Board for injuries caused by sexual harassment. This case was long and drawn out and many times I felt discouraged and depressed. . . . But I'm glad I took appropriate action against an intolerable situation. It feels so good to be a 'winner.' "

Your charge may help others in your company as well as yourself. And filing a well-publicized charge against one company may even produce speedy changes among other employers who want to avoid the same fate.

We do not yet have the basic rights as workers that we have as citizens. American corporations are not run democratically. We tolerate a lack of freedom in our jobs that would appall us in any other setting. When you sit down at your desk, you give up freedom of speech—you can be fired for what you say. You give up freedom of assembly—you can be fired for talking to other employees about the wrong things at the wrong time or for holding a meeting on company property. You give up freedom of the press—a leaflet or newsletter can be seized by your supervisor.

It is important that we exercise the rights that we do have and push to expand them, through action at the workplace, lobbying for improvements in the laws, and influencing the climate of public opinion that helps to determine how we are treated at work.

9.
Organizing: When Going It Alone Isn't Enough

Why did we form a union? We were given a handbook that said if we had any problems, we should go to the personnel office. But there *was* no personnel office.
—*University secretary*

The only thing I lost by becoming active was that awful helpless feeling.
—*Union steward*

THE movie *Norma Rae* tells the inspiring story of Crystal Lee Sutton, who led a breakthrough organizing drive in the modern-day textile industry. American labor history is full of Norma Raes. In fact, it was the militant actions of working women that started the modern labor movement early in the twentieth century. In 1909 New York shirtwaist factory workers, mainly women, carried out the "uprising of the 20,000," striking 500 shops. Three years later, 14,000 Massachusetts mill workers, mostly women, struck for three months in a bid for shorter hours and higher wages.

Observers are full of theories about why women office workers have not yet organized. Some say we're blinded by love for our bosses; some say male union leaders have neglected us; some say our employers crush our organizing efforts before they can succeed.

But no sector of society has ever organized overnight. The craft workers' unions were preceded by centuries of guilds. Teachers started associations in the mid-1850s but didn't unionize on a large scale until a hundred years later. Hospital-worker organizing, begun in 1919, didn't come to fruition until the 1950s. Public employees and nurses took gradual steps toward unionizing for fifty years.

When clerical work first emerged as an occupation, there was little need for office workers to organize. Wages, promotion opportunity, and working conditions were at the top of the heap. But in the past fifty years, office work and office workers have changed dramatically, and over the past decade our need to organize has become clear.

Our ranks have swelled while our pay has dropped to the low end of the scale. Our advancement opportunities are limited by discrimination and the structure of the clerical industries. We know now that the office is not free of health hazards. Automation threatens to degrade our jobs, if not eliminate them. As mothers of small children join the work force, we are squeezed between family responsibilities and unbending corporate policies. Our pension benefits are paltry.

And so, whether the theories about our lack of organization were right or wrong, they are rapidly becoming outmoded. Because of our urgent needs, women office workers *are* organizing. We are sharing information about job openings and raises; circulating petitions for improvements in job policies; meeting with management; forming staff councils, networks, coffee groups, and unions. Our history of organizing is beginning.

We are organizing for five good reasons.

First of all, it pays. To cite the strongest form of organization, women in unions earn 33% more than nonunion women. But organizing on a more informal level also pays. For example, one group of legal secretaries, each of whom had at least eight years of seniority, discovered that newly hired secretaries were earning nearly as much as they were. They held a number of meetings among themselves, researched salaries at other firms, and presented their findings in a memo to the senior law partners. By acting as a group, they won a new salary structure and an across-the-board adjustment. "If we'd gone in individually," one said later, "we'd have gotten nowhere."

Second, organizing works. There comes a point when a polite, private discussion with the boss is not enough. Individual office workers have been having polite discussions with bosses for fifty years, and our situation hasn't improved much. Speaking for many coworkers gives your views a legitimacy and power they wouldn't have if you spoke for yourself alone. One voice can be dismissed as that of a crank, but a boss can't easily ignore the chorus of voices from an entire department. Where an individual acting alone might have to resort to a lawsuit to protect her rights, many people working together can make such action unnecessary. Organizing is particularly effective when it results in a union contract, which requires management to negotiate over wages, hours, and working conditions.

Third, organizing is the professional thing to do. Doctors, teachers, lawyers, professors, actors, even bankers, recognize the value of association and have formed organizations ranging from informal networks to powerful unions with full bargaining rights. The argument that organizing is "blue-collar" and "beneath a white-collar worker" doesn't stand up. A written contract is nothing more than what many professionals insist upon before taking a job. And it's what most businessmen demand before they make any important commitment. Organizing is nothing more than an effort to protect your most important resource—yourself as a worker—in the most effective way possible.

At one institution facing financial difficulties, paychecks were ten days late each month while management collected the interest. One month, the office workers were asked to take two days of leave without pay. At the same time, automated equipment began to be introduced, and management boasted that within five years every office worker would be working at a video-display terminal. The office workers decided they needed a formal voice in the formidable decisions facing the institution and voted to unionize.

At the age of 60, Mary W., a librarian at a prestigious university, became an active member of a union. A few years earlier she had been vehement in her opposition to unions on college campuses, considering them undignified and unprofessional. When she had a grievance, she would put it in writing and send it to her superiors. After years of disregarded complaints and unanswered memos, she realized that far from compromising her professionalism, a union was the only way to preserve it. So, like professors, instructors, and other members of the university community, she now carries a union card.

Fourth, management is organized, and we should be too. Your boss may be a member of the Chamber of Commerce, the American Society for Personnel Administration, the Business Roundtable, the National Association of Manufacturers, and any of hundreds of industry associations and lobbying groups. Yet he expects you to shun organizing, "not just for the good of the company, but for your own good as well."

"Why didn't you come to me with your problems?" he

might ask a member of an organizing group. "If I had only known, I'm sure we could have worked this out one to one." Yet, if she had gone to speak to him alone, she might have found that rather than allow managers to handle problems on their own, the company had an elaborately organized system for dealing with matters of employment. "If it were up to me, I'd be happy to change the policy," her boss might have told her, "but I'm afraid it's up to Personnel."

Finally, organizing is satisfying. "It was nice to get the money," said one woman new to organizing, "but the best part was working together with people who used to be just faces at the water cooler."

As you become involved in organizing, you find yourself developing skills you never knew you had. You learn to chair a meeting, talk to strangers, speak to a crowd, and stand up to people in powerful positions. And as you find yourself meeting new challenges, your self-respect rises. "My boss used to refer to me as 'ten typing fingers,'" one secretary said. "Now we sit across the table and talk as equals."

Organizing among office workers takes many forms, ranging from informal groups of people within a single department to national groups comprising workers from many companies and many occupations. Here are the most common types:

Departmental and company-wide groups often begin with informal meetings to discuss such problems as an unfair office procedure or excessive work loads. Later, meetings might take place on a more regular basis, after work or at lunchtime, in the company cafeteria, a restaurant, or at someone's home. The groups can take up issues of concern to nonmanagement employees in many departments and can reach out to large numbers of employees. They are generally not officially recognizcd by management, except in the case of "employee advisory councils," which are formal bodies set up by the employer as a means of receiving ideas from employees. Representatives may be elected by employees or appointed by management. Decisions of such groups are not binding, and the employer often exerts considerable control over their activities.

Women's networks are composed of women from all levels of the company, including management, and usually meet monthly to enable women to exchange information and advise one another on routes to career development.

Outside support groups, like 9 to 5, function as support organizations for employees from many companies. They allow women to share ideas on career development and exchange effective tactics for improving personnel policies. They can publicize the concerns of women workers in the area and conduct public pressure campaigns urging particular employers to alter their employment policies.

Unions are associations of employees with the right to negotiate with management over pay and working conditions. The employer is legally bound to bargain with union representatives over employment issues and may not make decisions affecting employees' welfare on his own. Unions are the strongest form of organization and result in the most lasting improvements.

A union at a particular company does not have to be affiliated with any larger body, but most unions are. By pooling the resources of many workplaces, unions coordinate research, provide assistance for local needs, lobby, and share ideas. In turn, many of these established nationwide unions are affiliated with the American Federation of Labor–Council of Industrial Organizations (AFL-CIO).

Today, almost 7 million women are represented by labor unions, and women have accounted for nearly half the increase in union membership since 1960. Most women members of unions and associations are white-collar workers. In 1974 women from fifty-eight labor organizations organized the Coalition of Labor Union Women (CLUW). Through CLUW, women who are members of unions pool their resources to share skills and information and exert influence within the labor movement.

Suppose the office workers at your company have no organized group, and you would like to start one. Your strongest course may be to unionize. If you decide to take this route, you'll want to be sure to keep the early stages of organizing confidential. But if unionizing isn't feasible—for example, because your coworkers aren't ready—then you may opt for one of the less formal types of organization that office workers are involved in. No matter what your goals, many of the first steps of organizing are the same.

Where do you begin? If your office chair is uncomfortable, and the woman at the next desk has complained that her chair is also uncomfortable, then chances are you already have begun. Organizing begins when two or more people exchange common needs or grievances. But it doesn't stop there; an organization isn't effective until it begins to take action, and it doesn't begin to take action until the people involved recognize a common goal.

You must first identify the problems at your workplace and then seek out others who are also affected by them. Take note of everything that causes you dissatisfaction, and write it down if the list is long. Then go over the names of all the people in your office, department, or company, and check off those who have voiced similar complaints.

Arrange to meet one or two people at lunch and explain how you think a group could provide a means for working toward solutions. Ask for suggestions of others who might be interested. Don't worry about starting small. A group can begin with two or three people and end up as a force of several dozen or several hundred.

People join groups for varying reasons. For some employees, joining a group may be an opportunity just to discuss a few common problems, while others will be more interested in actually finding solutions to these problems. Still others will join simply because they like the other people involved and may drop out when the focus becomes less social and more active. Your aim is to include as many members as possible, so if the group is started by people from similar backgrounds and ages, make sure that its tone doesn't cause others to feel excluded.

Some employees will be less enthusiastic about joining a group than others. Many may want to wait on the sidelines until the group actually succeeds before committing themselves. Some will be fearful—of "destroying the friendly atmosphere," of "being too pushy," of limiting their individual flexibility. They'll advocate "giving management another chance." They may believe that management has their best interests at heart and will improve things on its own. For others, organizing may clash with their self-image. One woman says that she had to battle a powerful stereotype in starting her working women's network in Houston, Texas. "We're expected to behave like ladies here," she explained, "and we're not supposed to be angry."

Remember that different issues appeal to different people. One group of women found that their successful

fight for better maternity benefits left some of the older
women uninterested. They decided to campaign next for
a more generous sick-leave policy because of its broader
appeal.

Make sure, too, that your goals and the size or breadth
of your group are appropriate to each other. If your
problem is a simple one that affects only you personally,
you can probably solve it alone. But if your problem
affects many departments, try to reach everyone involved. At a large insurance firm, women in several
departments compared notes on their salaries and discovered many inequities between departments. They
asked for reclassifications and won raises and higher job
grades.

Your group will grow if you ask people to do things to
help carry out its goals. Few will volunteer; the more
active members of the group will have to encourage the
less active. Make sure the tasks are small, and appoint a
committee to accomplish something that might be too
large for one person—such as reading through the pension plan or calling women in several other departments. Also, keep in touch with people who aren't
willing to do anything yet. You and they should feel that
you are acting on their behalf, not just for yourself.

There are probably some people who will never be
persuaded to join you, but many reluctant coworkers
can be brought around if you respect their opinions.
"Keep the door open and others will come in," says one
woman who helped build a group that won new training
policies at her company.

In planning meetings of your group, keep in mind that
they have to compete with many other demands—family, job, TV, friends, housework—and if they don't accomplish anything or are boring, people won't come
back. Make sure each meeting has a plan, and prepare
concrete proposals for action ahead of time. No matter

how small your group, someone should chair the meeting to keep the discussion on track, let everyone be heard, and summarize what has been accomplished. Begin meetings promptly and keep them short—an hour and a half is enough.

Choose an appropriate place to meet. Many groups begin by meeting in the employees' cafeteria, but others find the atmosphere too intimidating and prefer someone's house, a coffee shop, or a bar. Make sure the ambience is one that all members of the group will find comfortable. If there are newcomers, make them feel welcome and bring them up to date by reporting on what happened at the last meeting.

Once you've identified one or more problems, people who care about them, and a means of meeting to discuss what to do, it's time to take action. Start off with a manageable goal. Even if what you really want is a total overhaul of the job-classification system or a union contract, you may want to warm up with something simple, like a new location for the coffee machine.

Not every group action has to involve meeting with management. For example, one legal secretary read a newspaper article about a 9 to 5 public hearing that detailed office workers' complaints about pay and promotion opportunity. She brought the article to work, underlined appropriate sentences, and persuaded as many as one-third of her coworkers to send copies to the law partners through the interoffice mail. Soon afterward came an across-the-board raise.

In another instance of creative organizing, clerical workers in a department at an insurance company were fed up with "oversupervision." Their supervisor patrolled the aisles between the desks like a guard. One day they all wore striped shirts to work. The supervisor got the message.

It's likely, however, that you will need to meet with

your employer to outline the problems that concern your group and to suggest solutions. You might begin by sending a memo to your boss to request a brief meeting. Gather your group to decide what you'll say and try to anticipate your employer's response.

At the meeting, describe the problem and propose solutions. Be prepared with several options you'd find acceptable. For example, instead of insisting upon immediate raises, you might be willing to settle for job upgradings or a new review schedule. End the meeting with specific requests—that the problem be fixed, or that an answer be given within two weeks.

After the meeting, report back to everyone about what went on. If your demands are met, publicize your achievement and move on to the next issue. If not, write a memo to your boss's superior and start the process over again.

Arriving at work one Monday morning, office workers at a small firm were amazed to find that one of the managers had a new secretary. Her predecessor had been fired without warning on Friday afternoon. "That day at lunch we decided to organize," Audrey Y. recounted. "We made arrangements to speak to the office manager and planned our strategy. We were scared and on edge, but we decided to act completely calm, and this gave us a sense of accomplishment.

"We made a proposal for a termination policy. We asked for written warnings and the right to appeal a termination decision to a mutually acceptable third party. And we asked that this policy be put in writing. The office manager listened to our proposals and said very little. But several weeks later a memo came out basically granting what we asked for."

If your appeals to management lead nowhere or if your boss won't meet with you at all, the time may have come to consider starting a union. If you choose this route—either right away or after trying some other options—the time is ripe. Many nationwide unions are increasingly interested in organizing women office workers. They are hiring women organizers and allocating resources to organize in the clerical field. As one AFL-CIO official put it, "American women are on the march. We want to join the march."

A sign of unions' openness to women office workers is District 925, a joint venture of 9 to 5 and the Service Employees International Union. In 1981, SEIU, an 800,000-member union, agreed to provide funding and other resources to organize office workers. The union worked in concert with 9 to 5 to reach out to office workers, offering both a firsthand knowledge of office workers' concerns and strong bargaining power. District 925 quickly broke new ground in many cities and now represents office workers from coast to coast.

The first step in starting a union is to call in an organizer. (For example, call District 925, SEIU, at 202-452-8750.) With his or her help, your group will form an organizing committee. You'll probably need to draw committee members from several departments; it's likely that your union will have to include all the clericals in your company, not just those in your own office.

The organizing committee will then ask employees to sign "authorization cards" which show interest in supporting the union or in having an election to decide whether to unionize.

Your boss can choose to recognize the union at any time, or he can demand an election to determine whether a majority of the eligible employees supports the union. Most elections are overseen by the National Labor Relations Board (NLRB), with some exceptions, particularly in public employment.

If a majority of the employees who vote supports the union, your legal relationship with management is dramatically changed. Employees can then work with union representatives to bargain for a written contract to improve wages, hours, job classifications, promotion procedures, vacation time, maternity leave, training programs, grievance procedures, and other working conditions. Management is bound by law to "bargain in good faith"—that is, to be willing to give and take.

It is worth noting that over 95% of union contracts are settled through discussion rather than through strikes, and it is this process that results in the substantially higher wages that unionized workers enjoy. Once the contract is signed, employees no longer have to mount a fresh struggle over the same problem again and again—many grievances are resolved once and for all. And the contract is renegotiated regularly, giving employees the opportunity to work toward improvements in its terms. If there is a dispute over the terms of the contract that cannot be resolved, management may no longer make the decision alone; an impartial third party can be called in to decide what is fair.

Dues vary depending on the union and are tax-deductible. In District 925, they are 1% of your salary with a ceiling of $15 per month. Dues go to provide trained staff, lawyers, researchers, lobbyists, and other resources.

How will your employer respond to your efforts to organize? Probably not with open arms. A typical employer feels threatened by the prospect of giving up control over personnel decisions and reacts to an employee group—whether union or not—with a strategy of his own. He may, for example, affect an air of nonchalance, but don't be fooled by this; the more he seems to ignore your activities, the more concerned he is likely to be.

Secretaries at a small insurance company circulated a petition that was intercepted by the boss. "You know what we do with these things?" he asked. "We throw them in the trash." And he was true to his word. A week later, however, he granted all their demands, including the abolition of a dress code applicable to women only.

Your employer may try giving one or two of you a raise or promotion while ignoring the substance of what you're asking for. "Take the promotion and keep on organizing," counsels one longtime organizer.

Some employers may seem to reform overnight. The president sends out a warm memo. The vice-president shows up at your meeting, professing sincere interest in what you're doing. Personnel hands out its own employee opinion survey after you've circulated yours. But such "nice guy" actions are often just tactics; your employer may have no intention of making changes.

Then there's the personal appeal. "Please give me one more chance," your boss might plead. "Don't join that group; I promise I'll be better." Only you can determine whether he deserves a second chance. Be aware, though, that this is an oft-used line.

Stalling is another common device you should watch out for. If you ask your boss for a meeting, he'll ask for some time to think about it and then when pressed will set a date for two or three weeks later. At the meeting he'll say he needs time to consider your proposals and will make reference to a consultant who will be brought in in a few months. The consultant's report will take a year to prepare.

Some companies are still more aggressive in their efforts to discourage organizing. Every week in some part of the country there is a management seminar being held, detailing methods for detecting telltale signs of union interest. A company that claims it can't afford new raises might willingly spend hundreds of thousands of dollars on anti-union consultants who tell them to beware of friendships among workers and, in one case, to "look out for a sense of direction among otherwise aimless employees."

Worse still, even though it's against the law, employers do fire employees for organizing. Your best protection is to act as a group and let your boss know that you are aware of your rights. According to one agent of the National Labor Relations Board, 90% of such firing cases are decided in favor of the employee.

In the end, though, your boss will probably give in. Most bosses do. Of course, he may make it appear that you had nothing to do with his decision to change policies. If the change itself is what's important to you, then let him take all the credit, but by now you probably have an investment in the principle of organizing and will want to let your fellow employees know that it pays off. In that case, commend management loudly for *taking your suggestion* and state your readiness to work hard to make the new policies a success.

Even if your employer is relatively compliant, it probably won't be easy to change your company's policies. Organizing is a skill, like typing or managing an office; it has to be learned over a period of time. Seek advice, if necessary, from trained organizers. If you are tempted to throw in the towel and go look for a job somewhere else, you may find that other companies won't be much of an improvement. Consider staying where you are and trying to make things better. You'll need patience and imagination, but if you do decide to persevere, you will be joining a proud tradition that has improved working conditions for millions of workers in every kind of job. The organized lobbying efforts of employees acting through their unions have made the crucial difference in the passage of the outstanding social reforms of this century—the eight-hour day, child-labor laws, minimum wage, Social Security, equal pay, and civil rights laws.

As one woman who made the choice to organize put it: "Aside from what I've gained personally, I feel that I'm repaying a debt to those who went before me. And I hope I'm making things better for those who come after me."

Gerry P. didn't consider herself a joiner. She went to a 9 to 5 meeting out of curiosity. "Once I was there listening to people talk about their problems," she said, "I realized how frustrated I was by my company's nineteenth-century attitudes." Gerry volunteered to look up some statistics for a report the group was working on, and "that was the beginning of getting involved. The organization made me proud of my skills. It brought out writing, speaking, and organizing abilities I had never been able to use on the job."

Gerry led a successful petition for job posting at her company, "but there were still a lot of problems. There were few job descriptions and no job evaluation process. Our salaries were among the lowest in the industry.

"Then management cut back on health benefits, which cost some of us seventy dollars a year. We wrote a letter to the president protesting the decision, and within a few days one hundred of the two hundred affected workers had signed it. But nothing changed. We never even got a response. That did it.

"We realized that despite our success with the job-posting petition, we had no rights. We decided to unionize. A group of us attended educational sessions after work and learned about the nuts and bolts of unionizing. Once we started the drive, more than sixty percent of the eligible employees signed cards in a week. We held the election and won.

"Now that we have a union, we're finally able to get

at the issues of professionalism and salaries that were so problematic in the past. In my case, I've been promoted and I've nearly doubled my salary.

"I'd like to see more women explore the possibility of unionizing," Gerry said. "History has shown that it's the only way that workers like us will be valued the way we should be."

Looking Ahead

WHAT does the future hold for women workers? Let's imagine the ideal office of tomorrow. We see women on every rung of the corporate ladder, treated with respect and paid fairly. Each of us has the opportunity to be trained and promoted throughout our careers. Office chairs are comfortable and the air is safe to breathe. New office machines enrich our jobs, freeing us from tedious work. The business world and society in general recognize the needs of working parents and their children, and the retirement system truly rewards us for our contributions. And finally, we have an ongoing say over our jobs, so that we may preserve and protect these ideal working conditions.

Will our dreams come true? Our growing numbers and importance will help us gather the strength to achieve our goals. For the rest of this century, the Department of Labor predicts, massive numbers of women will continue to swell the work force. This trend may well be the most significant in the United States' employment picture. The manufacturing sector will continue to decline, giving way first to the "paper economy" and then, with the rise of office automation, to the "paperless economy." Office work and office workers will become increasingly important in the economy of the future.

At the same time, however, we will face serious challenges. With the introduction of new technology, we may see the growth of an elite professional class in the office, separated by an unbridgeable chasm from the routine jobs most of us will hold. The "best" office jobs—those that involve variety, judgment, and contact with others—may disappear like an endangered species. Secretarial jobs may be upgraded, but there will be many fewer secretaries than there are today. Far fewer bosses will have personal secretaries to run their errands for them, and the code of etiquette that surrounds the serving of coffee in today's office may come to seem as quaint as the rules of courtly love in fourteenth-century France.

The increasing presence of toxic substances and stressful working conditions will pose ever-greater health risks to office workers. Only the rise of more humane ways of doing business can reduce these dangers.

As mothers continue to enter the work force, the need for family-oriented corporate and public policies will be more urgent than ever before.

How will these trends affect us? We could be buffeted by them, or we could take steps to shape our future and achieve the ideal working conditions that we can now only envision. No group of workers has ever influenced the course of history by sitting back and watching things happen. On a grand scale, we all need to stand up and ask for a raise—a raise in salary, a raise in status and working conditions, a raise in the ongoing control we have over our jobs. After all, we spend the majority of our waking time at work. We can't afford merely to put up with whatever happens to come along.

As isolated individuals we will never gain the power to bring about the changes we need. We'll need to join together in a strong organization that will stand behind us as we stand up for our jobs and our families. If we do join together, the 1980s and 1990s may be for office workers what the 1930s and 1940s were for industrial workers. In the 1930s factory work was the largest job category, as office work is today. Heavy industry was a profitable and healthy sector of the economy, as the white-collar industries are today. And factory workers performed difficult jobs for low pay, as do we. In the 1930s and 1940s, industrial workers organized in a great wave that won them higher pay, better benefits, and a wealth of social programs that benefited the entire work force.

It is likely that office workers will organize, and that we will win important changes not only for ourselves but for society as a whole. We will organize in our own way, with our own style and our own leadership. Today's union leadership will respond to the office workers' message. Women will move up through the ranks of union leadership, and unions will take up women's issues more than ever before.

In addition to bargaining for our rights across the mahogany desktop, we'll need to exercise power in the political arena as well. Many government policies have a critical impact on our daily working lives. Voting patterns in the early 1980s demonstrated the power of women, as we expressed our concerns for fairness, equality, and peace in significant numbers at the ballot box. Women—particularly working women—expressed views quite different from those of men, and this difference in voting patterns became known as the "gender gap." Pollsters attributed our different outlook in large measure to our experience in the workplace, where we are angered by our lack of power and lower salaries. Analysts noted that women are affected more than men by economic downturns; we are often the first to be laid off, and we are the main users of government assistance such as Aid to Families with Dependent Children, Medicaid, public housing, food stamps, and government legal services. Also recognized was the "compassion dimension" among women—a concern for others that expresses itself in a rejection of militarism, a respect for the environment, and a concern for the hungry and homeless.

The "gender gap" between men and women voters, significant as it is, will be more significant still if we more fully exercise our political power. There are 45 million women workers, but only a fraction of us vote. We must make it our business to find out about candidates for public office and evaluate their support for policies that improve our working lives. We must use our political muscle to insist that public officials outlaw discrimination, protect our health on the job, promote pay equity, guarantee a secure retirement, and help the working family.

It won't be easy. Employers aren't in business for their health. They will attempt to hold down every salary expenditure to protect profits and tighten every rule to increase productivity. And many will cling to their privileges for as long as they can.

Many of us will find it difficult to pursue better working conditions or to convince our coworkers to do likewise. "Sure, I'm fed up at work some days," you'll say, "but there's no sense making a federal case out of it. It's just the ways things are." A friend may advise, "If you don't like the way you're treated at this job, go find another." Or a coworker may argue, "Let's give management one more chance." In such cases, take the advice of a seasoned union organizer: "Keep an open mind, but don't let your brains fall out."

It may be financially risky and personally wearing to go out on a limb for an improvement in your work life. It's hard even to envision better treatment unless you've seen someone else work for it and succeed. Remember that we all set an example for one another. If you're putting up with a bad situation, you're encouraging your coworkers to put up with it too. But every time you speak up and take action, someone else will be inspired to follow suit.

When we organize to shape our future, when we proudly demand the working conditions that should be ours, we will succeed. The numbers are on our side, the need has never been greater, and our cause is just.

9 to 5, National Association of Working Women, would welcome you as a member. Complete this form and mail it to:

9 to 5, National Association of Working Women
1224 Huron Road
Cleveland, OH 44115
216-566-9308

_____I would like to join 9 to 5. Dues are $15 or $20 based on income.
    _____$15 (below $12,000)
    _____$20 ($12,000 and above)
_____My dues are enclosed; please send me information on starting a 9 to 5 chapter or becoming a local 9 to 5 representative.
_____Please send me more information on 9 to 5.

Name _____

Address _____

City/State _____ Zip _____

Phone (home) _____ (work) _____

Job title _____ Industry _____